HANK AND THE SNOWMAN

JIM SIDERS

outskirts press

Hank and the Snowman
All Rights Reserved.
Copyright © 2020 Jim Siders
v4.0

This is a work of fiction. Names, characters, businesses, places, events, locales, and incidents are either the products of the author's imagination or used in a fictitious manner. Any resemblance to actual persons, living or dead, or actual events is purely coincidental.

The opinions expressed in this manuscript are solely the opinions of the author and do not represent the opinions or thoughts of the publisher. The author has represented and warranted full ownership and/or legal right to publish all the materials in this book.

This book may not be reproduced, transmitted, or stored in whole or in part by any means, including graphic, electronic, or mechanical without the express written consent of the publisher except in the case of brief quotations embodied in critical articles and reviews.

Outskirts Press, Inc.
http://www.outskirtspress.com

ISBN: 978-1-9772-2055-4

Cover Photo © 2020 www.gettyimages.com.. All rights reserved - used with permission.

Outskirts Press and the "OP" logo are trademarks belonging to Outskirts Press, Inc.

PRINTED IN THE UNITED STATES OF AMERICA

Table of Contents

1. Life Is a Rollercoaster 1
2. Mom's Pregnant 3
3. The Hospital 9
4. The Silver Mine - and Then Some 12
5. Diary of a Cartel Boss 16
6. Evolution of a Punk 19
7. Hit Squad 22
8. Operation Seahorse 27
9. Nightshift 29
10. Hank the Toddler 33
11. Planting a Church 35
12. The Payoff 39
13. A Birthday Party 41
14. Not a Storybook Ending 44
15. Building the Network 45
16. You Can Run, But You Can't Hide 47
17. Physical Violence 51
18. Mean and Meaner Than Mean 54

19.	No Pain No Gain	57
20.	Mean Has Karma	59
21.	Funerals	61
22.	Hopscotch	64
23.	Identity Theft	69
24.	Like a Sore Thumb	71
25.	The Adventures of Moving	76
26.	Hank Returns to Scene of the Crime	81
27.	Hidden Treasure	87
28.	Point of No Return	94
29.	Water Scooter Investigation	96
30.	Connect the Dots	99
31.	Hank Talk	102
32.	The Marvel of T.V.	105
33.	Planting a Family	107
34.	Relocation	110
35.	Money Wire	116
36.	Time (Doesn't) Flies	119
37.	Mounting Evidence	121
38.	Special Customers	131
39.	Putting on a Show	136
40.	Special Education?	139
41.	SiriousXM	145
42.	iPhone to the Rescue	147
43.	Bang the Drum	150
44.	Christmas Shopping, Thank You PARA	152
45.	School Newsletter Editor	155

46. *Tragedy*..More Than a BeeGees Song 162
47. Ward of the State..168
48. A New Group of Friends.. 173
49. Show Me the Money..178
50. Vanishing Act 181
51. Row, Row, Row Your Boat 186
52. Doing Business at Business..193
53. Unexpected Encounter... 200
54. Awkward Meets Work 204
55. Reeder to the Rescue 206
56. Showdown at the OK Corral 209
57. Vigilante Justice 216
58. Rod the Rat..221
59. Rock, Paper, Scissors 225
60. Just Rewards 232

Prelude

I just love this book. Not necessarily because it is a good read, I really cannot read very well....because the book becomes my voice. My entire life, I have struggled to be understood. People discount my intelligence because they can't understand me. I have my own language that only a few people have been able to crack. Most people just think I am not smart and lack intelligence. You read and you be the judge. If you notice the font change to this type of lettering, you are communicating with me. My thoughts are my voice in this book and I hope you get to know me better than a lot of people.

My name is Hank and I wear a shirt and tie....because I can. Professional people wear a white shirt and tie to set them apart from everyone else. I believe in myself and I am proud of myself – so I wear a white shirt and tie. Once you finish reading this story and understand what I've endured, you may understand my fascination with white shirts and ties. Then again, you can read my story and may still not understand. If that is the case, I feel sorry for you. Don't judge this book (me) by its cover, judge me by what I achieved. When it is all said and done, I took care of myself and the white shirt and tie is my statement, since most people prejudge me.

People like me lose dignity and pride from our treatment by

"normal" people. If being normal is being ugly toward others, you can have it. I would have liked to have been able to play with the other kids growing up. I would have liked to have been invited into groups and had the same dances and romances....but I have cerebral palsy - CP. I cannot walk and really cannot talk, so this story is the best voice I have had in my life. I put up with everything, I struggled to move, and I cried when no one would give me a chance. Funny thing is, I got stronger with every failure and turned into the man with the white shirt and tie. Yep, I am proud and dignified.

1

Life Is a Rollercoaster

I can't speak for you......actually, I can't speak for myself, but sometimes they throw egg at you – and sometimes they throw the frying pan too. I look forward to letting you know about my travels, my trials, and my triumphs as you read this book. I appreciate Jim taking the time to put this together. My life has been anything but conventional and I have to be honest saying I am surprised I made it through everything.

A lot of people take it for granted when they get frustrated and complain about little things that annoy them. I sure do not want to dismiss any tragic events that some of you reading this book may have had to deal with. All I am saying is that I think I have had more than my share of tragedies and by the grace of God, I made it through. Most people are just having a bad day, week, even a month. They just gradually get over what is bothering them. Guess you could say they are having first world problems. Sometimes their bad day is an inconsistency in a very blessed life. They get over it. My bad days are linked to a pretty demanding life, I do not have the luxury of getting over my condition. I choose not to complain, but I have to admit, if people could realize how they treat me from my perspective, they would appreciate their first world issues.

I have experienced the greatest family (make that two families) as you will find out in this story. I wish I could go back in time and reconnect with them, particularly now that I have overcome all I have. Success is too often linked to what you have accumulated. My success is a part of what I have overcome and achieved even when life seemed impossible. So, come join me in this recount of the past 20 years.

The time is around Y2K….you remember that? Computers were going to go berserk when the turn of the century moved from 1999 to 2000. Civilization was set to crash because a bunch of techie nerds didn't think about programming code for computers having to adjust to a year like "000".

As it turned out, we geeked right past that end of civilization and most people marched right along on their merry way. Computer programming didn't throw me the curve I endured, but my life was a challenge from the minute I was born. Pretty amazing to sit here and share my challenges with you. As tough as it was struggling through my hazardous birth and the limited means by which my family lived – it seems pretty trivial when you consider how I had to deal with Faustino….THE SNOWMAN!!

Faustino just wouldn't go away. He would not leave me alone, even though he didn't know the crazy circumstance that would reunite us. No need for me to give away the ending, just take a read for yourself. In addition to ruining my life, The Snowman made me who I am.

Okay, I will bow out for the time being. Do one thing for me and my kind of people should you encounter "us". Show some courtesy in your conversation and think twice about making us invisible when you talk about us. Believe it or not, we have ears that hear and brains that think. Don't underestimate what we are capable of as you focus on what we cannot do. Take it from me and this story, "we" can do more than you can imagine. Best to you!

2

Mom's Pregnant

Carlos and LaNita were expecting their second child with the due date approaching in a week. The pregnancy was actually pretty smooth - no complications like the first child, Carmelita, who was accompanied by a lot of nausea. Such extreme morning sickness was just a tremendous struggle for a first-time mom. This was sooo different and much smoother, more relaxed.

Carlos and LaNita lived in the small village of El Ocaso bordering Medellin, Columbia. They waited for this day for nine months and were filled with joy for the miracle awaiting them. This bundle of humanity arrived in the early morning hours. The baby was a boy, Hendrick, who would grow to be called Hank around the house. They made the trip to the hospital in Bogotá in Carlos' broken down International pickup truck. The truck was more tin can and duct tape repair than it was truck, but Carlos somehow kept it running.

"This little one is coming Papi', so hurry up" shouted LaNita as she shook Carmelita from a deep sleep. The time was inconveniently just before 5 a.m.

"I will slide Carmelita in the storage behind our seat in the truck" replied Carlos.

LaNita clutched at her overnight bag in the seat next to Carlos as if it was an oversized stress ball. Her stomach and lower abdomen seized in pain. Carmelita woke up as soon as Carlos wrapped the blanket around her. Their little girl situated herself behind the bench seat in the small storage area and clung to her Mother's neck. LaNita wasn't really aware of Carmelita's presence with the intensifying contractions.

"Hang on Amor' " Carlos chanted mostly to help himself. Each contraction triggered a tighter grip on the satchel and more tension inside her womb. Every bump in the road amplified the discomfort LaNita was going through, "Carlos – smooth driving….PLEASE!!" As they drove along the bumpy road, LaNita thought about the local politicians' empty promises to improve the mountain trail this rickety old truck had to travel. Local roads and villages needed so much work and improvement. Now, as they bumped down the mountain trail of backwoods road, this couple sure wished they had gotten something back for their taxes.

Politicians tend to make hollow promises just to get in office. Gaining elected positions carried many benefits, but more lies than accomplishments. Genna Fortuna was very active in her church and community. Following two elections with promises to repair and fortify this lifeline of a gravel road and seeing no improvements, Genna decided to make a difference. She was the wrong gender to run for office, but her charisma and organizational skills would have been a difference maker if it was possible to qualify. Instead, she organized a strike more potent than any political promise….the women were going to "Cross their Legs" until repairs were made. Grandma's rule was eat your broccoli and you then can have your cookie. Genna's rule, fix the roads and the wives and the "women" would have sex. Medellin had a noted village brothel. Genna met with the various rings of prostitutes and the pimps. No one is sure how Genna got through the pimps, but the new "price structure" following the repairs to the roads was going to ramp up the price of service to make up for any lost revenue. Until repairs, things would get pretty testy and the pressure on the government would result in safe roads. At the moment, LaNita and Carlos did not see a safe road anywhere. Where was Genna when you needed her? Such was the lack of progress in a small village in Columbia – lost and forgotten.

Unfortunately, 5 miles from Medellin contractions started to set in deeper, longer, and in shorter intervals between pains. LaNita was consumed with her physical pain and couldn't imagine having any additional problems occurring. "Carlos, I think he is coming! What will we do?" With the anxiety mounting - the contraction shortening -and Carlos pretty much in a panic - Hank was about to be born out in the wilderness, absent a sanitary hospital room and the sterilized instruments.

Carlos thought his role in having a baby meant sleeping on a bed in the recovery room and whatever little baby congratulation cards would tell. He had no idea what he was to do in this situation.

LaNita began to scream and cry with pain and agony "Oh MY GOD…..stop the truck!!! Oh MY GOD….get me to the hospital!!!" Carlos just bore down on the accelerator and moved the junk truck along faster than was safe on this trail of a road. The frequent contractions were intensifying and coming quicker and quicker.

In all this panic, Carlos didn't need the ruts and washouts making the roads all but impossible to drive. Then……. the tire blew, the truck swerved to the left toward the cliff side of the road. "Oh Lord in Heaven, help us", cried Carlos. Then, as if by divine intervention, the rim of the front passenger tire dug into the dirt road, spun the truck perpendicular and launched it toward the hillside and away from a deadly trip down the mountainside. The beat-up International pickup lurched to a halt. Carlos jumped out of the truck as it butted up to the inside incline of the road and came to a halt. As the truck plunged into the side of the hill, the driver door flung wide-open and stayed ajar.

LaNita was screaming loudly, "Papi, help me, Lord God be with us!" No longer in control of the situation, well…..no longer thinking she was in control, Hank was beginning to crown. In these early morning hours - traffic on this pass was limited, which was good with the truck blocking most of the road.

For Carlos though, he couldn't pray harder for someone to come along. "Lord God, be with us, help us". As fate would have it, an employee of the local hospital was heading to work to start the 6 a.m. shift. Maldi Baldor, an Emergency Room nurse, saw the truck pinned to the side of the road bank. She screeched her car to a stop with the lights shining on the truck. She noticed the driver door open and expected to find the driver thrown from the truck and splattered against the hillside. Maldi always expected some type of calamity at the hospital but didn't expect trauma to find her here on the road.

Seeing the nurse approach in her white medical scrubs, Carlos thought he saw an angel. "thank you, Lord, thank you - Praise God. Mami' an angel is here to help. God is good!" Once he snapped back into the moment, he realized who Maldi was.

"Can I help you?" Maldi shouted.

He jumped out of the way allowing the nurse to take control of the situation. Maldi was looking for injuries from the accident. As surprised as she was to stumble upon the disabled truck, she wasn't really thinking about a baby being delivered.

"Are you hur…………." Maldi began to ask. Then she realized this wasn't an accident, it was worse. "Oh no" she said, as she saw the birth beginning to take place. Once nurse Maldi sized up the situation, she immediately assumed the role as a delivery nurse and began to facilitate Hank's birth. As Hank began his passage into the world, the nurse's jaw dropped open as she saw the umbilical cord wrapped around Hank's neck. "What else could go wrong?" she muttered to herself. She quickly loosened the cord and began to puff air into Hank. He showed limited response. Lacking any of the hospital equipment, the nurse began to bark orders "OK dad, keys are still in the ignition, pull my car over here to transfer these patients."

Carlos jumped in the car, pulled up alongside the beat up International. "I have a blanket in our travel bag" Carlos offered. He assisted LaNita while the nurse carried little Hank's body into the backseat of her car, mother and son still attached since she lacked sterilized instruments to sever the cord which had been clamped. Maldi wrapped the little baby in the blanket for warmth, "There, there little man, stay with us for a few more minutes. More help is waiting for you."

Maldi gradually took over more and more of the actions needed, "We need to walk together since I cannot separate mother and child. On my count of three, you hold up your wife and help her to walk - I will carry the baby. One, two, three"…..and they began the short but important journey to the car. Once the transfer had been made, Maldi directed Carmelita "okay big sister, we need you to sit in the front with your father and help him to see a clear path" as she, LaNita, and the baby squeezed into the back seat. "Let's not waste time."

Carlos worked the car around the truck coming oh so close to sliding down the cliff, then floored the accelerator pedal and flew down the trail toward the hospital. In the backseat Maldi tried to calm LaNita "What is your name? Just relax the best you can. Everything will be alright in a few minutes." Maldi carried on this conversation almost with herself, but it was calming for LaNita to have some assurance. The nurse provided assurance while simultaneously pumping vital oxygen into Hank's mouth and nose with a portable respiration device from her emergency kit.

With uncanny calm, Maldi shouldered her cell phone shouting commands ahead to the hospital to prep them for arrival. It was as if she had a split personality come in and out of the conversation to talk so softly and controlled with LaNita, then authoritative and loud dealing with the hospital staff. In almost unintelligible Spanish, Maldi barked out an explanation of the situation.

Upon arrival, the emergency crew greeted the car with a bassinet and a gurney placing the two patients into the respective hospital transports. Before moving any equipment inside, LaNita and Hank were situated on the gurney. The cord was quickly clamped tight and severed to separate mother and child. Hank had spent 35 minutes from crown to hospital with limited oxygen. Maldi and one orderly pushed Hank in his bassinet into one operating room while another orderly transported LaNita to her quarters. In hot pursuit of both transports Carlos and Carmelita chased the orderlies when suddenly they went two different directions. Bewildered - Carlos was left stranded in the hallway torn between two operating rooms. Carlos stood frozen and feeling even more helpless than before, not knowing which patient to attend to first. Finally, he felt the little tug of Carmelita's hand pulling him down the corridor toward LaNita.

3

The Hospital

Carlos and LaNita were united in her hospital room shortly after a doctor arrived. They shared a hug and prayer....then Dr. Santos broke the news to them. "Hello, I am Dr. Santos and I just left your little boy, Hendrick, in the Infant Intensive Care Unit." The unfortunate circumstances of the breakdown and roadside delivery combined with the reduction in oxygen would cost Hank quite a bit of motor response. "Your baby was placed in ICU to monitor response and development and to improve the oxygen available to him in his incubator." He had been deprived access to vital oxygen at the most critical point in life. "We anticipate your baby making it through this first phase, but it will be with some consequences. Your trip to the hospital was not the best circumstance, but Nurse Baldor did the best things possible in the situation. I cannot express how fortunate you were to have her stumble upon the scene when she did." The good news - Hank was alive; the bad news - Hank was going to deal with some degree of cerebral palsy the rest of his life. No doctor could predict at that moment how much cognitive damage had occurred. It was immediately clear that the transmission of motor command from the brain to muscles was going to be affected. Hank would depend on a wheelchair throughout his life. Carlos and LaNita, however, only heard the good news, Hank was alive.

LaNita was discharged from the hospital after two days to minimize costs. Hank, however, remained in the hospital in a special incubator for weeks in an attempt to minimize the trauma from his breathing. Hank actually had fair measures for his Apgar ratings. The Apgar is a 5-point scale used to make initial evaluation of a newborn based on color, cry, response to stimulation, etc. Without a doubt, he was going to be subject to a number of muscular limitations and inefficiencies with motion for the rest of his life.

Hank was quartered at the hospital where LaNita and big sister Carmelita provided daily support and tender care for his fragile physical existence. Carmelita quickly assumed the doting responsibilities of big sister and catered to Hank's every need. "Hi little Hank, I am so glad to meet you. I will help mommy take care of you. Love you Hank," she would say almost on the hour.

Carmelita reflected on the crash of the truck and scary delivery over and over. "Mami', was the wreck a dream I had? Everything happened so quickly. Was it a bad dream?" She was mesmerized by Maldi the nurse and admired her anytime she stopped by to check on her special delivery – Hank. "Hi nurse Maldi. You are so special. Thank you for taking care of Hank and helping us out." Despite her young age, Carmelita already knew she was going to grow up and be a nurse. She admired Maldi and watched closely during all procedures. "What are you doing? Why do you do that? Can I help you be a nurse?" She didn't ask why the sky was blue, but she asked almost every other question you could imagine.

Before Hank left the hospital, Carmelita was proficient in the routines that Hank needed to build the neural pathways as best they could develop from brain to muscles. Carmelita may have asked 1000 questions, but she learned from every interaction and observation. When momma finished feeding, it was Carmelita's job to put

Hank through his range of motion to preserve any muscle movement possible and to improve the reactions between brain and muscular network. LaNita was quick to praise her daughter for the interest and care she took to help little Hank.

4

The Silver Mine - and Then Some

LaNita, Carmelita, and Hank would remain at the hospital for weeks in order to stabilize Hank's condition. Carlos caught a ride back to the village with Maldi the second afternoon of the hospital stay. "How can I thank you for your help?" asked Carlos. "I shudder to think what would have happened if you had not appeared when you did."

Maldi replied, "Thank you Carlos. There is nothing you need to do for me and you really need not thank me. Providing medical care is my job and I am thankful I was there at the moment I was needed. I have to admit, that particular morning I was running behind schedule about 20 minutes and chose that mountain pass thinking it was shorter. I think we are all pretty lucky in that sense."

They rounded the corner of the trail and saw the old clunker of a truck still sitting in the embankment where it had rolled to a stop. The pitiful appearance of the truck was a security mechanism to prevent tampering or theft – who would bother with such a worthless looking truck. Once he reestablished himself at home, Carlos got help from a neighbor with a tractor to pull his truck back to the village and begin repairing the jalopy for local use. Maldi, the new guardian angel of the family realized the circumstance and assured Carlos "Please try not to think of the struggles and hardships. I will stay with LaNita and Hendrick every day I am on call." She further volunteered that once the baby stabilized and could be discharged, she would be the transport for LaNita and the kids to join him at their home.

"Thank you Maldi, you have been our savior", he replied. "Oh, we also decided that around the house, Hendrick will be Hank. You are part of our house and to you, he will also be Hank."

"Hank it is," replied Maldi.

Carlos immediately returned to his position in a local silver mine with the spiraling costs of medical bills hanging over his head. He had missed two full days in the silver mine and was told his position was gone if he missed another day in the next month.

"Where have you been Carlos? On second thought, I don't want to know and do not care. You're on a short leash now, one more absence this month and you are out of a job." Wow, nothing quite like a compassionate mine chief to lay a little more pressure on the situation.

Every time he entered the mine, he was preoccupied with the mounting fortune he needed to come up with to offset the debt. Neonatal Intensive Care was no part of the equation when LaNita and Carlos decided to have a second child. Dealing with next to nothing for an income, budgeting is pretty simple. Adding treatment for an infant in NICU and the follow up therapies, especially in an undeveloped community, was a recipe for financial disaster.

Extended stay in a hospital was going to break the bank pretty quickly. The NICU (Neonatal Intensive Care Unit) incubator, frequent pediatric care, and a pediatric physical therapist as well as occupational therapist resulted in much higher costs than Carlos could have imagined. In addition, the first few days after delivery LaNita and Carmelita were forced to stay in a hotel near the hospital. The hotel did offer weekly rates and a hospital discount, but the stay just added more to a mountain of debt no one saw coming. Every one of the doctors and therapists held true to "don't worry about the bills, focus on the baby". LaNita was consumed with Hank's needs and, living minute to minute, never considered the bill that would result for this extraordinary care. Carlos was removed from the scene, more objective, and much more aware that costs were spiraling out of control. The man of the house had to step up and provide and he would do everything in his power to care for his family – **EVERY-**thing!

Before long, Carlos hatched a plan and decided to take on a second job. Without elaboration Carlos explained to LaNita that he was beginning a second position and would be working late into the night. As LaNita moved from the shock of the experience on the side of the mountain and the impact of caring for Hank, she also began to gain an appreciation for the finances that these extreme measures had required. Both parents agreed that the financial burden of emergency delivery and continued care for Hank was beyond their meager lifestyle. There was no question that these parents loved Hank, nor could you doubt the extent that Carlos would go to provide care for this little fella. Sometimes, however, a dad needs to think twice before taking on just any kind of work. When pressed with the extreme expense combined with panic and emotion - Carlos was overwhelmed and lost all order of common sense. Little did Carlos realize that when he thought about putting his life in front of little Hank's, he was predicting the future.

Carlos' disregard of the second job as criminal activity was more a concern for survival than worrying about consequences. A distant cousin, Zeno, had been involved with the "Snowman", Faustino Carbona's drug cartel. The Carbona cartel was a small operation compared to many of the drug operations in full tilt during the 1980's. Faustino stumbled into the drug crowd during his teen years. He was a typically careless punk disenchanted with school and "above" legitimate work. Faustino was not about to start with some entry factory job or stoop to be a busboy in a restaurant. The hot drug commodity at the time was cocaine. The white powder reminded him of snow and as Faustino gradually grew his drug ring, he got enamored with himself and the success he perceived to befall him. He operated in the rural area surrounding El Ocaso. Faustino rationalized that this area was so far off the path that no one would look for illegal drug traffic of his minor scale compared to the real kingpins in major Columbian cities.

Carlos had a similar mindset to Faustino in one sense. Both decided that if they were to get caught by the authorities, they would develop a rationale of being too small an operator and had been taken advantage of by the bigger operations. Somehow that made sense to both men and justified their decisions. With each successful transaction, Faustino gained confidence. With confidence came greed and these ingredients fueled expansion of his operation. Carlos, on the other hand, was filled with fear to the point of nausea the first time he carried drugs. He never became comfortable but learned to live with his decision. It was for Hank.

The big boys were looking for small fries who could distance their business from the visibility of front-line distribution. The drug industry was really a huge pyramid scheme. People at the top not only skimmed the most money, they also structured the enterprise to hide themselves from lower level distributors. Key to building the pyramid was identification of an enterprising, young, reckless person that did not appear to think far enough ahead to connect the dots. These small fries typically lacked the smarts to head a cartel. Most of the underling operators thought more of themselves than was true. Faustino checked all the boxes, young, enterprising, reckless, and what seemed like a pretty shallow capacity to think. To cap it off, this cocky punk even coined his identity as *"The Snowman"* because he thought it would brand his operation in the drug community.

5

Diary of a Cartel Boss

Faustino's childhood - Del Toro was a small rough town to grow up in. Situated west of Medellin in Columbia, Del Toro was more poverty than anything else. Faustino was born in 1986, the last of eight children and wore the hand me downs of the hand me downs. He was the baby of the family but the target of his rough brothers. It was actually a good preparation for his future. As the baby of the family, Tino (so named by his siblings) learned to manipulate his parents and get what he wanted when he wanted. As the runt of the litter, Tino tended to get beatings from his brothers behind his parents' backs. At a very early time, Tino learned to be a salesman and learned how to talk his way out of trouble.

Maria, a local grandmother would take in all children if she saw the need. In the absence of a public pre-school, Maria ran a daycare for donations. Pay what you could or nothing at all if you couldn't. Maria simply liked children and maintained a bottomless level of energy to provide for the majority of children growing up in Del Toro. As a toddler, Tino benefited from time with Maria and other children served at the preschool. He seemed to be prepared academically for school, but school wasn't prepared for Tino. Even as a five-year-old, Faustino stole from other children at Maria's. One feature of Maria's curriculum was the introduction of spoken English for the children to gain a survival communication if called for. Little did she know what a foundation she provided for Tino.

He was a baby punk. Baby punks, new punks, seem to be predisposed to aggression and violence. Tino was aggressive with his stealing but most of that was the result of a missing personality filter. Maybe it got knocked out of him when his brothers would rough him up. Maybe it got ruined when his bark was bigger than his bite and older kids retaliated against losing lunch and school supplies. I imagine it was just impulsive, kid behavior that just went wrong - then went unchecked.

Maria enjoyed Tino's presence at her school, but she simply had too many toddlers and children to consistently address bad behavior. Impulsive 4 and 5-year-old behavior can be squashed by a teacher or adult. Squashing is not correcting and not correcting to extinguish a bad behavioral tendency tends to strengthen the behavior. Little Tino grew into these undesirable impulses which were left unchecked and not removed. Maria was doing good to squash behavior. Too many little kids like Tino get the squash treatment until the next opportunity to steal arises.... then bad conquers good. Flirting with but not correcting a behavior time after time ingrains a tendency that will typically get worse. Teachers and parents do not realize the damage they do when a temporary behavior fix ingrains to a personality disorder. Nip it in the bud with a little extra effort and you build a solid citizen. Suppress bad behavior and set the grounds for a predator in adulthood.

Tino carried this skill into his attendance at a local school. Tino was capable of hiding his theft from his teachers. Unfortunately, he wasn't skilled at selecting his victims. As in the case at most schools, Del Toro Elementary had its share of bullies. Tino unwittingly picked on Miguel as one of his victims. Miguel operated his own gang at school, he easily found out that Tino had stolen from his lunch pail. Recess for that particular day was not a good experience when Miguel cornered Faustino against a playground fence and basically beat him down. To make matters worse, Miguel made Tino give him his lunch for the next week. The lesson was learned and served more than that situation. Tino was temporarily out of business and suddenly a victim. Most kids would scare into straightening up. Tino stepped back and dissected Miguel's attack, penalty, and gang operation to sophisticate his own skill set. Bad, bad Tino and getting worse.

Thanks to Miguel, Tino became more discerning with his victims, and opted to pick on the little girls in his class. They did not push back, they did not retaliate, and they feared future consequences which prevented telling the teacher and parents. Tino learned who to pick on, who would help, and how to secure his profit. By the third grade Tino was a feared businessman. Playground terrorism is not the same as the community would come to experience from small gangs and organized crime. Playground terrorism in Del Toro Elementary was Tino's forte and he was good at being bad. Tino learned and refined these lessons for implementation as a young adult.

6

Evolution of a Punk

As he entered into adolescence, Tino turned into a phase 2 punk and his terrorist tendencies turned to manipulating innocent peers. One example was using a restroom pass in 8th grade. Tino took the opportunity to lite up a cigarette in the stall. Once things got smoked up beyond ignoring, Tino enticed an innocent boy in the hallway to enter. Once the kid entered to see a fictitious "you won't believe what is in there" ...Tino beat a path to a nearby classroom and ratted the kid out for smoking at school. The teacher stepped out of class and "caught" the smoker red handed. Tino the manipulator....WINNING!!

Trouble for Tino was no longer good enough for him to break the rules - now the challenge was to get someone else in trouble. Phase 2 Punks practice sophisticated aggression. The sophistication is the ability of framing unsuspecting others. School based terrorism in its cruelest form. Bad, bad Tino and getting worse.

Faustino fell into a pretty rough crowd during his senior years of schooling. This only served to pattern his adult livelihood as an aspiring drug lord. Faustino began using drugs at the age of 12 and saw a lucrative business to engage in. By the time he was 13, Tino had already determined that his desire to use drugs could be paid for by delivering drugs. He started at the ground floor and experienced every position in the drug distribution chain.

His business evolution was really pretty admirable, except this wasn't the supermarket stock boy working his way up the ladder. He worked as part of a crew initially. Tino saw his niche as a distribution network working among multiple drug gangs. Once he knew the players, he understood who to avoid, who to approach, and who to partner with. This drug business was similar to his experience with Miguel from the playground – sort of. Tino learned from mistakes and poor choices. But he learned and was very successful in a very short period of time.

Once he understood a source for his cocaine supplies and knew geographic boundaries from serving as a drug runner, he was setting up his own empire. He was a small fish in a big pond, but he was a fish. This local fish was making a name for himself in a poorly governed and loosely patrolled geography. When someone tried to cross Tino, just like ratting out the innocent 8th grader in the restroom, Tino made up a story to feed up the line and let the local kingpin dole out the punishment. Most of the victims didn't even know what they did to experience the attack they received. People started connecting the dots and traced things back to Tino after a few of his retaliations were launched. In short order, Tino began to strike fear in the users and fear led to respect. Respect fed up the chain of command and Tino was picked for more high profile and valued responsibilities within the drug enterprise. Higher profile with greater risk created more profitable reimbursements. Tino was on the rise and staking out his territory.

As he grew into his own, Tino was ruthless and got caught up in his image. Faustino thought a lot more of himself than many of the criminals he associated with. Most of his actions were barbaric, but he wanted to make sure everyone knew who was boss. In order to build his image, he controlled people through fear.

By the same token, many of his actions were really quite juvenile. Tino really never had good role models to follow. As his cocaine empire grew, he referred to the white powder as snow and he referred to himself as the "*Snowman*". Faustino even went so far as to ink his own Snowman tattoo on his forearm while doodling. He would repeatedly ink his design and ultimately began to embed ink into his skin with the pen he used for maintaining records. While most people who noticed the tattoo held back their snickers out of fear, it was pretty obvious that the design was not worthy of the pride Tino took in his art. The tattoo was his mark, but it was the work of an amateur. His snowman tattoo was not of quality and brought on a laugh from people not familiar with his type of terror.

As Faustino began to entrench himself in the drug circuit, he took note of the more prominent kingpins like el Chapo and Escobar. His idol, however, was the Panamanian commander Daniel Noriega. Tino was mesmerized by Noriega and his CIA affiliation. What a hero, a cartel leader that hoodwinked the United States of America. Drug cartel at its finest. Tino measured himself against Noriega and crafted his business in a similar manner. Noriega's chain of command and organization structure was analyzed, and *The Snowman* built his organization as a mirror image of the Panamanian drug lord.

7

Hit Squad

Faustino recruited and trained one of his brothers, Raul, to manage the hit squad of enforcers. Raul not only recruited his thugs, but also assessed the cruel attacks when a customer or cartel member dropped the ball or, worse yet, tried to game the structure for their own well-being. Exchanging drugs for money was just too loosely conducted not to have sticky fingers. Occasionally one of the runners would lift a hundred or a thousand bucks. No different than the cashier at a 7-11, it was too easy, it was too seductive, and face it.... the love of money is the root of all evil. Even evil within evil has its consequences. Raul and Tino were bad characters. They were the opposite of Tonto and the Lone Ranger - these guys wore black hats.

Raul developed his role as Faustino had by climbing up the ladder from the bottom. "It has come to my attention you took some of my money," Raul coldly explained to the culprit he had caught. As another member of the hit squad taped the culprit to a chair, Raul continued, "Now you must understand that I cannot have this going on. You will need to face the consequences. What would you like, pull out three fingernails or cut off one finger?" Raul would talk slowly and drag out the suspense to add to the agony. Regardless of the choice that was made, Raul would honor the choice on one hand, then conduct the other pain on the other limb. That first finger being chopped off, toenail pulled out, partial suffocation with the plastic bag...initially these were cringeworthy. Sooner or later Raul not only got used to the gruesome nature of his responsibilities, he began to develop an addiction to the emotional charge of inducing pain. Raul gained a sense of empowerment that accompanied the fear response of his victims. Not to condone the behavior, however, criminal acts of violence are widely documented. Studies of the Ted Bundy's, Charlie Manson, maybe even the abuse on the gymnasts by Dr. Larry Nassar. It starts small, grows incrementally, then you're hooked. Ironic that the addiction to "Snow" is consistent with the adrenalin addiction in violence. I mean really, you diet, you cheat with donut number one. You don't gain all your weight back over night, so you cheat again. The sugar high, the cocaine high, the Adrenalin high - they're universal in that it starts out in a controlled situation and escalates. Donuts hurt you, the Adrenalin rush hurts others. The comparison stops there.

Sometimes out of boredom, a guy can make a bad decision. As his operation grew and Faustino became increasingly distanced from exchanges, free time was in abundance and boredom ensued. Among the bad ideas that emerged was when Faustino created his tattoo of a snowman on his inner forearm. In his mind, it would be his badge of honor and to an extent, brand his drug chain. Who didn't draw on their arm in school when they were a kid. When you make your own tattoo as a kid, ironically, it looks like a kid's artwork. Fortunately for mom and dad, those eventually wash off.

So, here is Tino using an old pen to embed ink under his skin without a pattern or design to follow. His "tattoo" quickly became disproportioned and look like "kid's artwork". Unfortunately, Faustino did a good job of creating a permanent image on his forearm. The do-it-yourself tattoo looked really amateur when he finally decided it was complete. This homemade effort to brand his business definitely set him apart. This type of distinction, however, was not what he had hoped for. Faustino developed a pretty short fuse with his critics, particularly those that snickered or laughed out loud at his artwork. The beatings and physical retaliation he doled out, soon replaced his tattoo as his reputation.

The Snowman built his image upline. This Snowman tattoo remained a joke among the established cartels instead of a signature of success. When meeting with associates of other distributors, he was always outmanned and knew better than to instigate a fight. Funny how things unfold, Faustino was actually recruited by multiple cartels to transact business in order to distance themselves from identification by police. The goofy tattoo of a distorted snowman led the bigger operators to size Faustino up as a simpleton and scapegoat that wouldn't be able to defend himself if caught. In his mind, Faustino was protecting himself since he wasn't aligned with any single cartel. Contrary to his poor logic, if the authorities did triangulate operations, Faustino would appear as one of those consistent names that would be mistaken as a kingpin. Tino made sure to beat someone with enough consistency that fear was the brand instead of the silly tattoo.

The Snowman was growing his operation quickly by working across so many different cartel lines. While he did not come across as one of the sharper tools in the shed, Faustino was street smart. In addition to feeding his ego, he became more credible as his operation grew. He realized how important he was as the low fruit on someone else's pyramid to buffer a cartel from the authorities. Tino finally had his "aha" moment and began to recruit his own tier of protection the same way he had been recruited.

Once he realized the potential in his own drug chain, Tino quickly became addicted to wealth. Street smart or dumb luck, it really didn't matter because the bigger operations got most of the attention. A combination of location, location, location (remote countryside) and being a small fish compared to the "el Chapos" of the drug world provided Tino with enough shelter to fly under cover and unnoticed. Small fish was still starting to see the money roll in. Faustino was into money and money was power and power was identity. Tino had made the scene, at least in his mind.

Faustino met with Raul to have some drinks one afternoon. "Raul, we need to take the next step. We need to keep the business going under these other operators, but it is time for me to be an operator," Faustino talked down to his brother. Raul was older than Tino, but he had gradually come to realize, Faustino was in charge.

"What do you plan to do? Raul asked. "What is wrong with the way things are now?"

"I didn't bring you here to question me, I am telling you, we are going to go on our own. Now, if that is not good enough for you, walk out now, but always look over your shoulder." Tino shot back at Raul. "Are you with me, or do you think you can make your own life? Oh, the answer is NO".

Things shifted quickly and Faustino explained his plan to rent some local farms to begin growing his own supply of drugs. Raul sat back and took it in. He really did not like a little brother telling him what to do, but it was clear his little brother was telling him what to do.

The growth of *Snowman's* business was gradual and controlled, but the way in which he pitched his offers to local farmers only left one answer and that was "Yes, I would be glad to work with you." Knowing the source as they did, the targeted farmers knew that if they did not comply, their entire family was in jeopardy. Tino would use 1/3 of their acreage and match their income from the other 2/3 of the farm. Of course, Tino got the prime fields to grow, but the landowner was going to come out better than before. That was about the extent of the good in the request. One farmer after another fell in line when provided the "opportunity".

As the "grow your own" philosophy took hold, Faustino found

himself frequently meeting among a variety of people from different walks of life. One situation that always bothered him was when he encountered "customers" from other nationalities that did not speak Spanish, particularly from the United States. The Snowman did not like to be dependent on anyone, particularly Yankees who used their own interpreters. Tino wanted to maintain control and he surely did not like to be subject to someone explaining his plans and policies to one of those hombres from the U.S. No telling what the interpreter was feeding him and vice versa.

In order to build his language versatility, Tino began to buy programming in English to watch on television. His favorite tutor was the "I Love Lucy" series. He had to concentrate on the spoken English in the program but was entertained by the humor that characterized much of each episode. Throw in Ricky Ricardo with his Spanish dialect and Faustino was smitten with this teaching medium. English wasn't all that bad when Lucy and Ricky were dishing things out. Tino became pretty versatile in English speaking and listening, but he never was able to shake his heavy Latino accent.

8

Operation Seahorse

Faustino had become intrigued with deep sea fishing once his drug dealing had matured and provided him the means for his extravagant lifestyle. Tino had a personal boat captain that would plot courses and find challenging fish adventures in the Gulf of Mexico. Not a month would pass that Faustino had not taken to the sea for his escape from the constant concern with law enforcement. The pressure had mounted over the last three years with assistance from the United States to reign in the drug business which was wreaking havoc from coast to coast. Faustino knew the time would come when he would have to flee to save his life - his fishing excursions served two purposes. The wealth that accompanies a successful life of crime with drugs is unfathomable. Extravagant purchases were just part of the lifestyle. One peculiar fascination Faustino had was a fleet of four Yamaha 500Li Sea Scooters. These Metalic Black/Green machines were very sleek, but dark enough to not stand out in the water or sitting on the deck of the boat. One could easily conclude that the sea scooters and scuba gear served to enhance his fishing trips. At $1800 per scooter, it was a little hard to appreciate owning a fleet of 4, particularly when you were the only person making any use of them. Chalk it up to rich AND selfish. So why not throw in an extra battery for $725 so you could flip the power in and out and not wait on a charge. *The Snowman* and money have no boundaries, you have it – you spend it.

Tino would suit up after a few hours of fishing from his boat and dip into the ocean alongside his scooter. His routine amounted to approximately 30 minutes of cruising 10-15 feet below ocean surface. The battery pack he used for the scooter had an hour and a half charge. Keeping an eye on his watch, Tino prompted himself, "well, well, time to turn this around. Let's see if the gps can find my boat." Tino needed to get used to returning to the ship and finding his "mobile home" within the restricted time frame. There was a method to his madness and the rehearsal would mean a lot when needed.

A few more toys Tino used for these scooter trips included a waterproof gps on his wrist. Initially, he could practice returning to his fishing boat by hitting home on his mapping device. Google Maps and similar tools will automatically show you the way home on a trip. Tino got used to his gps navigator regardless of where he was in the water. Even if he had meandered around reefs or underwater landmarks, when called upon, the "Home" directive provided him a straight line back to the boat. The other essential tool was a timer for his other wrist. Time was initially more important than direction since the battery packs had a limited life expectancy. After the 30-minute mark, the potential to be stranded at sea rose exponentially. Tool number three was a walkie talkie with a quarter mile broadcast. In the event he did not make it HOME, he had a capacity to call for help. "Hey captain, check your sonar for my signal and see if you can find me" he would occasionally request. Again, this was planning for the future and testing his network of tools. His weight belt contained a sonar signal that would assist the boat captain in his search to find Tino. Lost at sea in the waves is the worst kind of "needle in a haystack" search you could imagine. Without the gps, searchable signals, and communication, getting lost in deep water was a distinct possibility. Tino needed to be adept at incorporating all his tools to limit the chance of becoming shark bait.

9

Nightshift

Carlos was the first to leave the hospital and had to bide time by himself. He had toiled in the mines and always just made enough for family needs. His reality was more sober than the rest of the family. LaNita never really gave thought to financing any of the household, she just made things work. Carlos, on the other hand, realized that the medical expenses were more than what LaNita could just make work.

Carlos needed a cash infusion. Living in a location like El Ocaso did not provide work options. Most people scraped out a means of survival growing their own food and occasionally trading vegetables in Medellin if clothes or other needs existed. Carlos was aware a distant cousin, Zeno, had become involved in a local cartel operated by this fictitious person - *The Snowman*. Tino thought himself to be more a Zorro type, but he was the only person with that sense of purpose. In the village of El Ocaso, drug operations were a major source of fear. Community members built up Faustino's reputation as *The Snowman* and placed him on the same pedestal of concern as El Chopo and other drug operators.

After much thought and anguish, Carlos decided to use Zeno's contact as an approach to *The Snowman* with hopes of capitalizing on the lucrative crime ring as a drug runner. Functioning as a mule to transport the drugs seemed like the least involved position on the ladder of consequences. After all, Carlos would not have daily contact with Tino and could distance himself from the decision making and authority of transacting drug trade. In his mind, Carlos figured that being removed from actually pricing drugs would isolate him from the consequences. If ever he was caught, the lies would flow free. Carlos would cooperate if and when necessary by explaining he really knew nothing of the activity. Every load he transacted would always be the first and only time. He would just be a pawn duped into something that seemed too good to be true, but too good to pass up. This was to provide for Hank and his family, and Carlos rationalized that everything would be dumped on someone else if he ever got caught.

Carlos and LaNita were both deeply religious and regarded their belief as a pillar of their life. Carlos prayed fervently and daily for God's forgiveness for his step into this dark side of life. Carlos prayed that one day he would escape Tino and the drug dealing but considered Hank his priority and justified his decision to provide care. LaNita and Carlos regarded Hank as their special gift from God, but his medical demands were on their minds every single day. LaNita and Carlos gradually overcame the extreme resources required of Hank once the second job helped with costs. LaNita never caught on to the unexplainable amounts of money pouring in to cover medical expenses and Carlos was not about to reveal the source. Carlos maintained his meager lifestyle. He gave no pretense of his extra income from the drug trade to anyone in his tight village community.

Carlos thought through his new responsibilities and arrived at a novel way to disguise the cargo he was expected to deliver. First, he needed a container that would fit in his truck bed. He wanted something that would be air and watertight to protect the packages of drugs he would transport. While visiting a local market he stumbled upon some crates that would sit in the truck bed and leave a full foot of space above the top edge of the container. Construction of the crates was pretty sturdy in order to accommodate stacking them while containing fruits and vegetables that need not get crushed. Each crate was lined in plastic to further preserve the contents.

In order to facilitate placement and retrieval of the crates, Carlos built a wooden sleeve that could easily store two crates. A tarp was draped over the sleeve and anchored to a tiedown on the base of the truck bed at both corners of the cab with a rope threaded into eyelets in the tarp. The tarp was drawn up over the wooden sleeve then tucked between the sleeve and the passenger wall of the bed. The sleeve opening faced the tailgate which was covered by the tarp draping over the end of the sleeve. This end of the tarp was held in place by another length of rope threaded through another tiedown on the floor of the bed just inside the tailgate and opposite the cargo sleeve. The pull rope was looped through a series of eyelets on the fringe of the tarp with another four feet of the cord extending past the tarp. Another tiedown at the top of the bed wall inside the tailgate received the end of the rope on the passenger side where the cargo sleeve was situated. This assembly was designed to protect the cargo sleeve and drugs from the "elements".

All the protections were put in place to allow for the camouflage Carlos was going to place over the bed and the sleeve to deter anyone from examining the truck. Carlos had a lot going for him to distract the authorities by virtue of the run-down appearance of the pickup. Icing the cake, so to speak, he shoveled a 6-inch layer of dirt over the tarp creating a slope of the dirt over the cargo sleeve. Now, the "elements" were heaped over the dirt as Carlos shoveled chicken manure 6 to 8 inches deep throughout the bed. He stood the shovel on a 45 degree lean against the shallow side of the chicken droppings opposite the cargo sleeve. In addition to most people being hesitant to dig around in the mess covering everything, most people couldn't manage the stench of the manure. This portable farmyard gave rise to Carlos' nickname within the drug circle as "el Tufo" - the stink.

In order to retrieve the drugs from the cargo hold, Carlos would drop the tailgate. The gate was clinging to the hinges and supported by a chain longer than called for and made the gate dangle downward from the bed. This was not by design, but the downward angle of the gate allowed any "elements" to fall away from the bed to keep the drugs clean when pulled from the sleeve. After swinging the tailgate open, Carlos could pull on the rope at the top of the bed wall and raise the canvas. One or both crates could be retrieved from the sleeve and emptied out for the drug exchange. Payment was received and placed in the crate to be hidden from authorities. In the ten years that Carlos provided drug drops, no one ever bothered to stop and inspect this stinky rattletrap truck.

Unlike many of the drug mules that worked for *The Snowman,* Carlos was dependable and honest. He was not comfortable with most of the shady characters he delivered to, but he had confidence that fear of Faustino would protect him from injury or theft. Carlos didn't tamper with the payments and always returned the full amount for the exchange. In a short amount of time, the volume of the exchanges increased as confidence in "el Tufo" improved. Carlos was reimbursed handsomely as his cargo value increased. *The Snowman* understood the need to differentiate pay as the amount of drug and risk increased. If he was crossed, Faustino made an example of the reckless, sticky-fingered mule. First offense was a severe beating when money was missing. Second offense typically resulted in loss of some of those sticky fingers. Occasionally, a runner would dip into the till a third time and those occasions led to a missing person's report. One would think the beating would send a message, but one does not think in the same way these roughnecks would. Carlos had things figured out as long as he was going to engage in this line of work.

10

Hank the Toddler

LaNita and Carlos were very supportive of their children but raising a little boy with cerebral palsy was foreign to both parents. Hank could cry – oh could he cry – but neither parent was able to make the connection between any event or function their son needed or expressed and his sounds. They were much like everyone else. LaNita continued to dote on Hank as if he was still a newborn even though he was approaching his second year. Mom did not really mind doing anything Hank needed, if only she could figure out what it was. She did notice different squeals, grunts, and moans that Hank would make, but it never impressed on her that certain sounds may distinguish one need from another. Big sister Carmelita was LaNita's right hand helper and Hank's number one fan. Carmelita was inseparable when it came to Hank and did not mind handling any responsibilities. Even when it came to changing dirty diapers, she was a trooper and performed these least desirable chores with a smile and hug to make sure Hank realized how much Carmelita loved him.

Maybe it was the difference in perspective from being a daughter and not a mother, but Carmelita gradually came to realize that Hank was communicating. In addition to the different sounds he made and the tones, Carmelita noticed a change in posture that Hank would attempt while suspended in his little sling stroller. Sometimes Hank would rear back and push his head into the back of the stroller pushing his bootie off the seat. Other occasions, she would notice Hank rocking back and forth in his stroller or shifting side to side. Over time, Carmelita noted how Hank might pair a sound or tone with the rocking or shifting. She did note how crazy it was that Hank always had a smile on his face. Sometimes he might gag on his meal, other times he may soil his diaper, and often he would drop something he was playing with, although his toy selection was pretty primitive. Regardless of the need, Hank knew how to work for attention and more and more often, Carmelita was the first responder.

Matching Hank's sounds and motions, Carmelita began to make predictions of what Hank needed. Thirsty, hungry, toilet, sick, pain — all had their own combinations of sound and movement. Over time, Carmelita was able to put together a system that Hank was teaching her. Not bad for a two-year-old to be able to develop and teach communication to family members. Not bad at all when everyone treated Hank like a toy lacking intelligence resulting in no expectations from him whatsoever.

11

Planting a Church

"Carlos mi amor', I want the children to have a wholesome childhood. I think we need to find a church to attend," LaNita encouraged.

"What do you have in mind my darling" replied Carlos.

"I have heard that a new church community is going to develop in La Quiebra. Can you travel there and find out more?" she asked.

"I will make a trip over this weekend and see what is developing. I look forward to building my faith with you," Carlos chimed in.

LaNita had been raised in a home that embraced the Christian religion and read systematically from the Bible. Carlos had a wholesome upbringing and had learned to respect his family and neighbors, but not within the structure of a religious affiliation. When the couple united as one, Carlos was quick to adapt to LaNita's wishes to raise the family within the Ten Commandments and to respect God and His Son Jesus. Her belief was cobbled together from family tradition rather than a church structure. Neither LaNita nor Carlos had been raised in a community large enough to support a church or faith community. When the word of a pending church assembly circulated within the mountain communities, LaNita and Carlos were eager to join in with this development coming to nearby La Quiebra.

Seth and Lorraine Grissom had been commissioned from Arisen

Son Church in Tuscaloosa, Alabama to plant a church in a remote countryside bordering Medellin, Columbia. The Grissoms responded to the calling for international ministry. Grissoms never had children but had enough family experience through the church to fulfill their desire for children. Seth and Lorraine realized they had passed a reasonable age for their own kids and were starting to feel their version of empty nesting. They felt their lives needed a renewed purpose.

Lorraine had pulled together the paperwork to apply for international service and Seth began the process of building their eligibility to relocate and represent the church. Following reviews and on location visits to La Quiebra, Columbia, the appointment was made for the Grissom ministry to plant a church. Church plants require time to build a congregation, establish a physical location, and construct the facility. Seth and Lorraine were on a five-year timeline to get this up and running and develop a clergy team to hand the church to upon their completion. Understanding the language to a degree of fluency was critical to their success. Both Grissoms knew some Spanish but immersing themselves in the community would be the only way to understand and utilize the dialect. Step one was to become physically present with the people and Seth and Lorraine establish patterns of walks they would complete daily; morning, afternoon, and evening. Walks turned in to meet and greet opportunities in a short period of time.

As Seth became more conversant with the people, he was able to share the Word and invite people to their home for brief services. Before long, five different services were scheduled on Sundays over the course of the day and new groups were appointed on Saturdays. The first step was to build consistency in the small groups. Most of the women in La Quiebra were home makers and Lorraine began to organize daily events for ladies interested to fortify the home environments. This two-pronged approach was very successful to accomplish goals for the first year. A distant relative of LaNita's had taken a keen interest in this developing church and mentioned the availability to LaNita in one of their rare communications. Carlos and LaNita, despite the 30 plus mile journey, became regular members. They began making the family trip from El Ocaso for Sunday afternoon Bible studies.

While some church members were surprised with Hank's physical condition, they took to Hank quite readily. Most encounters were pretty pitiful and more an act of sympathy, but everyone found a way to meet Hank and engage him in their limited ways. Carlos and his family became active members of the church. They cared for other families just as other families cared for them. People meant well and wanted to befriend Hank, but they just did not understand his condition and lacked the insight to reach beyond the communication barrier. While Seth and Lorraine were not professionally prepared to interact and engage Hank, they quickly realized their capacity was far greater than any of the locals.

Year 2 continued the success and realized four men interested in pastoral leadership for the church plant. Seth met with these four teams two nights a week and slowly integrated each into Sunday services for five, then ten, and fifteen-minute messages. Many of the men had construction skills and contributed to the erection of the church. Carlos found time one late afternoon a week to contribute to the construction effort and began to make friends with different people. Carlos needed this community and he understood that more than anyone.

In addition to the delivery of worship services, the church became a very popular community center. The four-member clergy team was taking ownership and began to diversify their outreach based upon individual personality and interest. Individual family support had the greatest impact in the community as team members met and prayed with families experiencing illness, tragedy, and life consequence. The outreach of the church was far and wide. Not surprisingly, relatives of church goers would be invited to attend small groups, worship services, and prayer supports.

12

The Payoff

Carlos made the numerous payments to the hospital over 10 years. Every week, however, Carlos also deposited money under a loose piece of the floor in his bedroom. As he deposited extra sums of money into the canister "bank" below the floorboard, he dreamed of the time when this risk would be behind him. Hank was maturing and became very aware of his surroundings. Ironically, everyone had decided Hank was incompetent as a result of his inability to speak words. His parents decided Hank possessed no intelligence as a result of his cerebral palsy. Hank, on the other hand, was very aware of all activity in the house and knew that Dad was doing something very curious in his room.

Hank the patient, did not seem to be much of a risk to understand how dangerous this second job was for the family. Carlos was cautious and by deliberately minimizing his lifestyle, he deflected attention from his life of crime. Driven by his pride and determination, Carlos put away his extra income to pay down every penny of Hank's bill. Much to LaNita's pleasure, the hospital bill was cleared, and Carlos announced his intent to scale back to his original job in the silver mine. At last he could put his life of crime in the rear-view mirror and have a normal life. At least that was what Carlos thought.

Carlos innocently requested a meeting with Raul, Tino's brother, and shared his resignation as a drug runner. Carlos very graciously thanked Raul for the opportunity and the relief the racketeering brought his family. The meeting quickly moved from a discussion to an ultimatum. Raul explained that there was no way Carlos was ever leaving the cartel, at least not alive. Raul told Carlos to rest assured that his pickup and drug delivery that evening was going to go down or he would face the consequences. This side job would have left little doubt of the consequences for most people, but Carlos did not understand how deep into the cartel he had drifted. In the ten years of paying down the hospital, Carlos had become counted on to deliver larger and larger drug shipments. Carlos was really quite naïve about the risk to his life and his family as a result of his service as the drug mule.

Carlos knew what he had to do and respected his belief in God to take care of the situation. Carlos was committed to escaping the clutches of this criminal activity and despite the fear for his own life, he was adamant with Raul about his resignation and building a distance from the cartel. Raul moved within inches of his face and screamed at Carlos with a forceful tone that anyone else would cave into. Raul ordered Carlos to leave and reinforced the necessity for Carlos to take the run tonight.

13

A Birthday Party

That afternoon, rather than picking up the package for delivery for the "Snowman", Carlos went home to celebrate Hank's tenth birthday. What a great day to be alive! Hank was going to turn ten years old today. LaNita was prepping for a family birthday party and had scraped together the ingredients for a cake. While she was busy cooking in the small kitchen, Carmelita was busy taking care of Hank. Carmelita had double duty today. On top of watching Hank, she found time to create decorations like the **HAPPY BIRTH-DAY** banner cut from discarded newspapers collected from the neighborhood. She made a special hat for Hank to wear by folding a sheet of newsprint into a cap like she learned at school. Her hat, like Mom and Dad's, would be the tall funnel hats made by pinching the corner of a sheet then rolling the opposite side in a large circle to create a cylinder. More paper was used to chop up small flakes of confetti to throw in the air. Streamers were fashioned from strips of paper that she would curl by pulling a scissor blade down the strip to make it roll. LaNita had taught her how to curl ribbons when they wrapped Christmas presents each December.

Carlos had carved out some funding from his dual income streams before walking away from the cartel. The hospital bills had been paid in full and a cash reserve had been built up in the hiding place below the floor in their bedroom. This was an opportunity to splurge that would mark a big change in the family. He wanted Hank to have something that could entertain him. Carlos had purchased a battery powered radio for Hank's birthday. Extra batteries were made available to keep the tunes flowing when the first charge ran out. Carlos had checked the reception before wrapping the gift and despite their remote location, found a few channels of music that could be received remarkably clear. He didn't understand the dynamics of radio frequency, but the elevation of their home on the mountainside made for a clear reception of the stations in nearby Medellin. Carlos made some presets of stations that he felt would lift Hank throughout the day. He would show Carmelita the operation and she could be a disc jockey of sorts and locate the best choices that she and Hank would enjoy. Carlos envisioned little Carmelita dancing to the tunes and spinning Hank in his wheelchair to engage him in the listening. They would love this special gift.

Carlos took a shower, cleaned himself up, and put on his Sunday best to join the celebration. Everyone was about to settle in for a wonderful celebration. Mom, dad, and sister were so proud of Hank and appreciated his consistently happy outlook despite the physical limitations imposed on him. LaNita situated the birthday cake in the front room on the table serving as their dining area. Big sister had put on her special dress preparing for the celebration of Hank's life. Hank was beaming inside, but little change in emotion was noticeable due to his CP. Carmelita knew to look in his eyes, she could see his soul on fire through his gaze and had learned to receive communications from Hank from this passageway. Hank thought to himself *"what a lucky person I am to have a Carmelita. If I need an arm, she becomes my arm, if I need to move, Carmelita is my leg, if I need to be understood, she is my mouthpiece".*

Candles were lit, they gathered around the table, sang the birthday song, and cut the cake. Everyone got an oversized slice of cake and laughed while reminiscing the life of Hank. Hank reflected to himself, "*How lucky I am to have this wonderful family. This is what love is. Papi provides for us and me in particular. I could have been a burden to other fathers, but Papi always found a way to get us by. Mami' always had a cheerful tune she would sing while cooking and cleaning, she is my butterfly – so lovely. And Carmelita, who could ask for a better sister. Over the years she had developed a system of communicating with me and come to a point of finishing my thoughts. Almost like magic she would know my hunger, my discomfort, my every need. Some of the stinky poop I left her with was plenty of incentive to predict my needs, but if she misjudged or did not notice my squirming, she never complained when dealing with the stink. My Carmi, my life!*"

As a result of his cerebral palsy, Hank flailed his arms wildly as he tried to muster up breath to blow out the candles. Due to the diminished muscle control, Hank could not even collect the air needed to extinguish the candles. Carmelita joined little brother in the ceremony and assisted in blowing out the candles. Hank's arms were flying everywhere as he tried to shovel the cake into his mouth. More icing and cake was smeared on Hank's face compared to what made it inside his mouth. The family sang "Happy Birthday" to Hank and then gave him his present. Hank tore paper for what seemed like an eternity. Carmelita and LaNita constantly offered help then finally reached in to provide assistance. Despite the danger surrounding the decision to exit the cartel, Carlos indulged in this storybook opportunity without thinking of his "job".

14

NOT A STORYBOOK ENDING

Not long after opening the gift, a knock was at the door. Fearing the worst, Carlos cautiously opened the door. To a certain extent, Carlos was relieved by his cousin Zeno standing and waiting to enter. Carlos hesitated, then invited Zeno in and took him back to the kitchen. Zeno quietly explained the course Carlos had to take. His family had to pack light or not at all and get out of town fast. This was not a question or request; this was a command.

Carlos wasn't sure what to do. He processed the situation thinking that it would come down to a showdown between Raul and himself and only himself. In fact, Carlos had gone so far as to take out a small life insurance policy years ago to cover himself if this type tragedy occurred. The full consequences of his life of crime never crossed his mind; he suddenly realized he may have placed his entire family in jeopardy. Cousin Zeno knew he was risking his own life by speaking with Carlos. Zeno quickly departed.

Carlos tried to maintain calm and asked LaNita to start to get things ready to leave. LaNita was confused and struggled to understand what was going on. When the fear in Carlos converted to tears, no questions needed answers, toiletries and clothes were thrown in a bag for an escape.

15

Building the Network

Well, what did Carlos have to be concerned about? It was after the fact that he caught on to the risk he had placed his entire family into. Carlos really felt that when his finances had stabilized, he would be able to thank Faustino and move along. Carlos thought all people had some good in them and that Tino would be rational. Those assumptions were so far off mark and Carlos was beginning to realize he would really have to assert himself if he wanted out of the drug business.

Tino grew into the monster he had become. His ability to rationalize good from bad flew out the window as the money poured in. The longer you live a life of crime and get away with it, the stronger the tendency is to become careless. Month after month of pushing drugs through the remote Columbian mountain villages gave rise to a sense of invulnerability. Tino could feel it, he was becoming smarter than the authorities – at least in his mind. As time passed and *The Snowman* remained at large, Tino's confidence began to swell.

Tino and his cartel were ruthless, vicious enforcers. The top of the chain of this group knew how to spread fear and fear was power. Any one of the underlings in Tino's ranks who showed any inclination to revolt or refuse a command was mercilessly taken care of. Ultimately, these "traitors" were killed, but not before a violent, painful beating of some sort in the presence of innocent bystanders and a few new hands in the drug chain. It was extremely important to Tino to maintain control by instilling the most brutal assault imaginable. Once his ranks began to formalize, Tino stepped away from the assaults and put brother Raul in charge. Raul was wicked. He incorporated a variety of painful techniques to instigate the most fear possible. Partial strangulations, multiple cuts and mutilations with a knife, strapping and dragging victims behind a vehicle, and "all of the above" would be used to maximize suffering for any person suspected of turning on *The Snowman*. Sad as their suffering was, the target was ultimately killed, but only after prolonged agony and in front of an audience. Raul was very skilled at his craft and this served Tino well.

This is what happened to Carlos and his family. Word got out that Carlos wanted out and was going to go straight. Tino and Raul decided to personally intervene. Since it was Carlos and he could serve as a caution to other families in the community, they decided on a "family" intervention.

16

You Can Run, But You Can't Hide

******Spoiler alert, spoiler alert**........this chapter addresses some extremely violent actions against my family. Jim and I decided to caution you - that you may want to skip a couple of chapters knowing that my world was stripped from me. If so, I suggest you check the Table of Contents and go to Chapter 18. If you do read this chapter and 17, try to keep in mind – I had never experienced an attack on another person. I had been raised in my home and cared for by two great parents and a super sister. Try to read from the standpoint of my innocent shoes.

Jim did a great job of capturing the attack, I prefer not to think of it, but it has been ingrained in my brain. We were cautioned about sharing the detail of three murders. Providing the degree of detail was intentional because Faustino and his brother, Raul, had terrorized Columbia and had been escalating their attacks in the past year. The way that they killed my family served one important function, the horror they inflicted galvanized the community and the law enforcement to finally take action. The devastation against my family unleashed an effort to bring The Snowman to justice which resulted in a $2 million bounty placed on his capture....... **Dead or Alive.**

Other readers suggested that we spare you the details and Jim *did just that. Maybe give it a try, but please do not hesitate to jump forward to Chapter 18 with the knowledge that Faustino - The Snowman, and Raul, had grossly overstepped their bounds. The hunter had turned into the hunted.*

Before they had a chance to get anything to the car, a screeching customized Avalanche pickup slid to a halt. They roared up to Carlos' house, cut the engine and had feet on the ground before the truck had a chance to stop running. They burst through the front door with little effort. Homes in this area weren't built with security in mind, pretty much a flimsy barrier of protection from the weather.

BOOM !! – the door flew open. The victims in this case were mostly innocents. Carlos knew the risks - well, knew there were risks. But LaNita, Carmelita, and Hank were blindsided by the attack. It's one thing to be aware and cautious, it is an entirely different trauma being attacked out of the blue. The fear is almost unfathomable. The shock is unreal. You don't have a chance to experience that sinking feeling - you just sink like Alice in Wonderland falling down the hole.

First Raul went after Carlos and knocked him cold with the second strike of his gun handle. Faustino dove and contained LaNita with his elbow jammed into her back with his full body weight amplifying her pain. She was quickly shackled to a chair by the ankles with zip ties.

Raul quickly attended to Carmelita as she tried to blindly run into an adjacent bedroom. There was no way out other than the door which Tino now blocked. He grabbed hold of her and dragged her back to the front room by her hair as she writhed violently against his grip.

Hank was frozen in his wheelchair. As the shock subsided, Hank began to rock himself back and forth trying to free himself from the chair, his trusted chair - his only form of mobility. He could feel himself inch his buttocks toward the front lip of his seat, but this positioning only limited his movement. Faustino grabbed Hank under his left armpit and shoved him back in the seat. Effortlessly controlling the youngster helped Tino decide not to waste any binding on him. Hank was going nowhere. Hank did, however, see that crazy Snowman tattoo as Faustino wrestled him back into his chair. Whatever that was, it was forever etched in Hank's mind. He couldn't make any sense of the image on Tino's inner forearm, but the tattoo quickly transitioned from that arm to Hank's eyes, to Hank's memory. He didn't realize it, but Hank had a terrible case of Snowman on the brain.

Tino and Raul wrestled Carlos into a chair. While LaNita and Carmelita screamed and cried for them to stop, Raul tied Carlos' hands behind the chair and taped his ankles to the chair legs. Any sane criminal would have gagged Carlos. Sanity was not a primary quality of Tino's. He purposely left his mouth free to scream out the pleas for help. Tino was no normal criminal…he was pure mean and leaning toward insanity.

Hank and Carmelita were traumatized and frozen with the assault taking place on their parents. Carmelita suddenly broke from the fear and decided to run. While Raul lunged at Carmelita to prevent her escape, LaNita flew into a rage and lunged at Raul dragging the chair behind her. Tino jumped up from Carlos' ankles and grabbed LaNita. One quick punch to the jaw and LaNita was officially the second prisoner. The contact with LaNita was no slap across the face, this was a haymaker that a heavyweight boxing champion would be proud of. The plan was made in advance to grab the kids after binding the parents so that Carlos would have to be the audience to the murder of his wife and their children.

LaNita was blindfolded and bound so she could hear the children scream for their lives.

The intent was to maximize the trauma to the parents and have them witness the torture of their children. Then, following her execution LaNita would be carved up in front of Carlos to insult his manhood as protector of the family.

Carmelita's attempt to escape out the front door was cut short when Raul grabbed hold of her. Tino finally shoved a piece of clothing into Carlos' mouth because he was actually starting to embolden LaNita with the contempt displayed toward the attackers. Veins in his forehead looked as if they would burst from the rise in Carlos' blood pressure. His anger and now the restraint of his voice only seemed to build his inner strength.

Suddenly, the action shifted to restraining LaNita. While Tino pulled Carmelita to a sofa and zipped her ankles and arms, Raul dragged LaNita to the couch, fashioned her arms around Carmelita's waist and zipped her wrists together. In so doing, he forced LaNita to hug her daughter. Raul wanted to make his attack on Carmelita the worst experience for LaNita by joining her to Carmelita for forced observation of the pending torture. He contorted LaNita's body into a painful position by zipping her ankles to the stubby legs of the couch.

Act one - terrorizing Carmelita. While anchored to her mother, the violence began. Raul made cuts to the back of her legs behind her knees. This was part pain and part agonizing bloodletting. Then they began manipulating her fingers with knives. First piercing the tips of her fingers to distribute pain from her lower torso to her fingers. Time to remove LaNita's blindfold so she can see the terror in her daughter's face. She lost a lot of blood in their violent attack. LaNita was in shock and the pain subsided as adrenaline kicked into gear, she thought…." this cannot be real".

17

Physical Violence

Carlos was going crazy with the attacks on his family. He had rocked the chair back and forth doing anything to break the binding holding him captive to the chair. Having to witness the torture to LaNita, Carlos had turned his chair over. With his legs taped to the chair legs and arms roped down at his sides, Carlos's head took much of the impact as he tipped to the floor.

The crack of his head on the wooden floor actually made him black out for an instant. He dreaded having to watch another member of the family be butchered by these madmen.

Raul returned to Carlos and bound him to a support column on the side of the room. He bound his hands together behind the beam to prevent him from breaking loose. Carlos had no leverage and was stuck. Carlos was beginning to realize how this was going to unfold. It was obvious that the agony of a slow, torturous action was going to be witnessed by Carlos before they took the real matters into hand to kill him. Part of the planned agony was to force Carlos to see his family killed in front of him. First, before more violence to his wife and children, Raul and Tino pulled Carlos' legs separately behind the column. For their leverage, they shoved their feet against his face or ribcage to pull legs simultaneously. Carlos was a human turkey wishbone and excruciating pain was inflicted by dislocating at least one hip in the process. The pain was beyond anything Carlos had ever experienced. Unfortunately, it was only the beginning. Carlos' head drooped to his chest in an effort to minimize the pressure on his hips.

Carlos began apologizing to his wife and children while pleading mercilessly with Tino and Raul. "Take me and let them go. They did nothing, they know nothing. Please let them go. They will never tell; they don't know you." His plea was worthless. Once the action began, the drug culture dictates that you take no prisoners. You just make examples.

Suddenly, Raul jammed his fist into Carlos' chest sliding it up under his chin forcing his head back against the column. Tino reached from behind the pole and began to run duct tape over Carlos' forehead around the pole. For good measure, he ran a couple of lengths of tape under his chin and around the pole. Finally, Raul pulled Carlos' top eyelids up and flipped them inside out while Tino taped his eyes open. Carlos could not escape this theatre of horror.

Hank was still petrified with fear which grew each time one of his family shouted in agony. "Please, stop, please!" While Carmelita shouted, "Papi, help me, Papi" Hank ran the same thought through his mind. Hank thought *"Why? What is going on? Stop! Help me Papi!"* Screams and cries rang out every 5 seconds. Hank had never seen anything close to this assault - this violence. His brain was going haywire. *"What was going on? Why?"* Hank's torture included not being able to express himself to the family. Hank observed helplessly in silence as tears welled up in his eyes and streamed down his cheeks.

The ultimate insult was when Tino informed Carlos that Hank was going to be spared his life, but the caveat was Hank alone by himself with his extreme limits in ability. Carlos' final thoughts were focused on Hank being stranded and dying a slow death of starvation. Then, Tino began to take Carlos from this world with his own hands as he choked him within a breath of life, let up, then choked him again, over and over to agonize him. Finally, after his 10th episode, he pulled a plastic bag over Carlos' head to suffocate him. Tino pinched three small holes in the bag over Carlos' forehead to allow the least amount of air in to perpetuate the sense of suffocation.

18

Mean and Meaner Than Mean

Tino turned his attention to Hank next. He spoke to Hank with very deliberate words to explain what had happened. Hank had a clear picture of Tino seared in his mind. A long scar down his left cheek seemed to point to a single tattoo on his arm. The tattoo was a snowman and seemed so out of place for such a mean person. The snowman was not very lifelike. Tino's snowman was like a cartoon creature instead of what most tattoos looked like. Hank could not get past how out of context the tattoo was for the evil that carried it. The scar and the tattoo would be etched in Hank's mind for as long he lived, which suddenly did not seem long.

Long torture to a ten-year-old confined to a wheelchair probably meant something different to Hank than the rest of the world. Hank had already gone without a lot as a result of his disability, the poverty he lived in, the hard life associated with a family of a mine worker, and the incapacity to speak and be understood…this little boy lived on very little.

Tino was determined to reduce Hank's primitive existence to another level. He wheeled Hank to the center of the room. After determining the farthest location from Hank, Tino moved the small kitchen table and put an unpeeled banana out of Hank's reach for Hank to dream about eating. Taunting him with out of reach food was as cruel as the butcher shop they had already delivered. Tino took the time to talk to Hank as if he were wishing him goodbye. This goodbye was more like a death wish. "And now leettle bambino boy, you weel get veery hungree. You weel get veery thirstee. And you weel scream for help, but no waan weel heelp you." Tino actually taunted Hank and ridiculed his condition. "Leetle creepuhl boy, you weel die a veery slow deeth. Cry for uuncal Tino, leetle waan, cry and I weel let you free." Just like anything else to come out of his mouth, this was a lie. Tino wouldn't have thrown Hank a rope if he had one dangling from his hand.

The gravity of this move was hard to comprehend. Hank processed the world and life differently from us. He depended on someone to push his chair where he wanted to go, so effectively the food was out of reach even if it was next to him. If he could reach it on his own, peeling the banana was beyond Hank's ability. Hank had come to understand how to guide his arms to an object, but he couldn't maintain the positioning long enough to grab hold. He had actually become quite adept at moving objects to a location like a wall or table leg in order to brace himself. He could contain an object by stabilizing his reach and grasp against an immovable object such as the wall. Coordinating both arms, however, to peel the banana wouldn't have been any more difficult than if he also had to flap his arms to fly....it just wasn't going to happen. But none of that was as pressing for Hank as the torture of the family.

Meanwhile, Raul, had been outdoors to look out for any passersby to make sure no witnesses would be present. Raul entered the house and tripped in the front door from a small threshold not showing above the makeshift ramp built to help Hank. This small stumble seemed to throw Raul into a rage (as if he wasn't already at rage and a half) and blame his misstep on Hank – after all, it was his ramp. Raul caught his balance, lunged forward, and backhanded

Hank across the face. The blow was enough to knock Hank out of his wheelchair while the chair remained upright.

Hank actually fell into the large pool of blood that had finally trickled out of his mother.

He was so distraught with the clear knowledge that momma was dead, Carmelita was dead, and dad was gone - he just lay in the blood and cried. Nothing really mattered to Hank.

Suddenly, a rattletrap car roared past the home and spooked Tino and Raul. They ducked out the front door to escape sight in the event anyone was actually nearby. Raul had not thought about closing the front door when he stumbled in. The rattletrap car turned out to be Zeno.

Recognizing the Avalanche pickup as Tino's, he was not about to stop and try to disrupt something he knew was beyond his capacity. Zeno drove past the house.

19

No Pain No Gain

As quick as it started, their fun stopped. How the police knew to show up at such a remote homesite wasn't clear. What was clear was the need to leave. Cousin Zeno didn't stop to help out Carlos, but he did place a call tipping the police to what was surely a pending slaughter. Tino and Raul were no amateurs when it came to violence. Their revenge and enforcement would typically be carried out with no witness, no link to themselves, and usually no way of getting caught. How the authorities knew to show up at this isolated house was a total surprise to them, but it only hastened their departure. Police announce their arrival with sirens blaring to alert innocent bystanders to make way. The sirens also alerted Tino and Raul. Both of these heartless barbarics knew they needed to move and not be engaged in a gunfight. Each of them drew pistols and began shooting the three family members who were already dead, but why not make sure.

Hank had pretty much turned into wallpaper with his inability to move. He was sprawled out on the floor in horror as the last breaths of life vanished from every member of his family. As he watched Raul and Faustino run out the front door, he continued to sob. All he could do is lay in bewilderment and confusion. His entire world just vanished. *"What just happened?"* he thought.

Hank was beside himself with grief and confusion. Covered in blood and beginning to realize how endangered he was, Hank began to attempt a crude crawl toward the front door. Really this was more a roll than a crawl, but Hank was going to fight with the same resolve his dad had shown. Papi worked this dangerous second job to satisfy the bills for Hank. Now, Hank was determined to find help one way or another.

Just as quick as the two drug lords left, the police ran in. They froze at the sight of the multiple murders. They actually didn't realize Hank was alive for a few minutes as he was filled with fear and laying lifeless on the floor next to his chair. Finally, one of the police noticed him and realized he was alive. The officer picked him up and removed Hank from the scene of the crime. He carried Hank out the door, called for another officer to retrieve the wheelchair, and placed this near lifeless little boy in his transport.

"There, there little boy, this was a terrible thing that you saw" the officer said. "I know you will survive this. Do you have a nearby relative?" he asked. The officer attempted to console him, but Hank's inability to talk left man and child in an awkward stare down. With not a single close relative to step up, Hank was taken to the police station to stay for the immediate frame of time. Adding insult to injury, Hank was provided a bed in a remote jail cell to stay until formal arrangements could be made through the Department of Child Safety.

20

Mean Has Karma

Tino had joined in on this "enforcement" to make sure the lesson hit home, and word definitely got around. But the message circulating was that *the Snowman* had gone too far with the torture and death of Carlos, LaNita, and Carmelita. As upsetting as it was, the authorities realized that Hank was exposed to this harm to his entire family and then left helpless and all alone. As gruesome as the attack was on his family, exposing Hank to the torture and forcing him to helplessly endure everything was a calculated cruelty. Something significant had to be done to Faustino for this travesty. He had gone too far, and his sense of invincibility had gotten the best of him.

Authorities had returned to the scene a day later to analyze what had occurred and gather evidence for a formal investigation. The murder scene was so grotesque and horrific. Even seasoned forensic specialists had difficulty ignoring the brutality that had taken place. Coupled with the horror was an anonymous call from Carlos' cousin Zeno that pointed the finger directly at *The Snowman* as the perpetrator. Word immediately circulated through the local villages that these murders were the work of Tino. The hunt was on and this madman had to be brought to justice.

Faustino realized that this time his payback was not going to be tolerated. The entire hillside and all local authorities were fed up with the violence, this family execution was simply too much to ignore. Tino knew he needed to leave the country. An intricate escape plan had been developed over years for this very situation. Operation Seahorse was set into action.

The authorities were on the hunt for Tino and it was time to flip the script. Local police intended to make a statement with his capture. Tino knew too well it was not just a matter of if he was going to be pursued, but when. Regardless of his growing sense of confidence, *the Snowman* knew the heat would eventually be applied and he was not about to melt. Tino sent message across border after border to enact the escape plan he had so meticulously orchestrated.

First, Tino had to look different. *The Snowman* was bigtime enough to warrant some international attention and a disguise was in order. Step one, his dark hair and ponytail were gone. A buzz cut and blond hair dye did the trick. He had a pair of black horn-rimmed glasses with fake lenses to wear once he arrived at his destination. He also had a single eyepatch to put over one eye if he had to enter into anyplace that may employ facial recognition software. A wad of gauze in his cheek would further distort his features if he was concerned about technology. Where he was going, loose, non-descript beach clothes would contrast his standard Khaki slacks and starched shirts. With his increasing wealth, Tino had developed a desire for business casual clothes to distinguish him from his poverty-stricken neighbors and associates. He gave thought to a nose ring but decided against something that might make his new identity too outlandish. He did change a pierced ear from a diamond stud to naked ear. Gold chains around the neck and gaudy rings were left behind and replaced with a cheap Casio wristwatch that would complement his beach look. Cheap all white tourist sneakers substituted for his rich taste in fine leather boots. Tino stepped back from the mirror and looked at his new self. He couldn't help but smile at the bum looking back at him.

21

Funerals

The assembly from the church planted by the Grissoms came together on a Saturday rather than Sunday to pay homage to the family they had lost to *The Snowman*. Lorraine had made way to the patrol station to retrieve Hank from his peculiar living quarters. She stopped and bought Hank a new set of clothes, his first white shirt and tie, while her husband prepared for the funeral service. Seth opened the service by reflecting on the lives of Carlos, LaNita, and Carmelita as well as to recognize the need to support the remaining member, Hank. This was a closed casket and because of the circumstances, the three family members were to be buried in a single casket. Nothing could be done to mask the gruesome details of the attack which altered the appearance of each person. Hank was still in shock from the brutal assault and inability to freely express himself.

Oh dear Papi' and Mami', how can I live without you? Hank thought to himself. *And my best friend, my sister, my support, where are you now, I miss you so much. I need all of you and I want to be with you.*

Seth opened the ceremony with a prayer for the deceased to be received in Heaven. Carlos had contributed a significant amount of time in the construction of the church and was widely respected for his efforts, regardless of the apparent ties to the drug cartel.

"Lord, it is with great sadness in our hearts that we lift these three dear members of our family up to your care" prayed Seth. "Let us remember each of these lost lives for the valued church members they had become. Lord, also shine your gaze on Hank, suddenly left on his own with little means for support and the demanding life he leads. Amen."

Seth then shared a brief statement about individual testimony and the recognition that it is never too late to receive the gift of life from Jesus as Carlos illustrated. Carlos was 42 years old when he had a formal opportunity to understand Jesus and to declare his faith in Christ. Seth also spoke of the open invitation everyone shared to receive life through Christ regardless of background and sin. Seth relied on Carlos' plight to preach of forgiveness and overcoming the many tests that life provides.

Lord take me to be with my family. I have nothing now and no reason to live, **Hank thought to himself.** *How am I to survive? I am so lost, help me Lord, help me.*

As if by divine intervention, the next words from Seth's mouth provided an answer. "As believers, we have a responsibility to one another. We look out for each other as if no boundary separates one family from another in Christ's family. For the immediate time being, Lorraine and I will take Hank into our home and provide for him as his family would have done. If anyone feels a calling to provide this care in our place, do not hesitate to speak now or contact me in the immediate future." Even LaNita's distant relative failed to declare Hank as a family member. The congregation was unable to see how they could provide for this young boy with so many special demands.

Seth stepped up to meet Hank's immediate needs of food, shelter, and clothing. Initially, Hank was a visitor to Lorraine and Seth. Within months it became clear that the Grissoms needed Hank as much as Hank needed them. This little fella was heartbroken and devastated by the death of his family. To observe such violence imposed on his entire world was going to take a long time to digest. Lorraine was every bit the mama and developed routines to meet his needs and actually provided for Hank better than he had ever experienced. Seth always made sure to involve Hank in events and find ways to engage him with church members in more depth than LaNita and Carlos had been able to perform. LaNita, in particular, was a doting mom and with Carmelita interested in helping her little brother, they had created a sense of entitlement by Hank. Even the best intentions have consequences and Hank was a fish out of water without sister and mom. Carlos was just as over the top with Hank, but he was not around nearly as much and only by absence, was less a detriment to Hank's development.

Seth was on a mission to make Hank as independent as possible. After sizing up the situation for a month, it was obvious Hank needed to have a process to communicate and express his needs. Following a regular routine of visits to Medellin for research at the university library, Seth had some ideas to create a communication board for Hank.

22

Hopscotch

Now that Faustino did not look like himself, he undertook the first leg of his escape plan. Before departing, one key communication was made to a confidante within his organization of dealers. This person was to initiate a series of contacts who would be critical to his escape out of Columbia. He selected one of his more dependable off-road motorcycles from a small fleet he maintained at his home. Not knowing whether the authorities had already begun their search for *The Snowman*, a trail he had made for a trail bike was his exit route. With a small bag of clothing strapped to the carrier behind his seat on the motorcycle, he ripped through the overgrown vegetation following an internal map he developed from numerous trips from home to Turbo, a coastal town. His clothing bag included some supplies he would need to begin a water journey out of Columbia.

The Snowman made his journey along the coasts of Central America and into the US. His chain of command had identified and chartered a series of fishing boats and yachts to anchor a mile offshore at select locations by latitude and longitude. *The Snowman* had created an escape waterway using these boats as rest stops at select gps settings. Once Tino made it to each boat at a location 1/2 mile from the maritime boundary of one country, the captains had agreed to release *The Snowman* to the opposite maritime boundary at a half mile marker. Tino used his water scooter from one water "Uber" to the next. At the half mile location, Snowman dropped the water scooter into the ocean and using his gps, rode the mile of battery he had to the next water Uber. This planning had to be pretty precise or Tino was going be stranded and turn into fish bait in the middle of the Gulf of Mexico. After his jungle journey from Medellin to Turbo, *The Snowman* decided it was best to eliminate his trail by switching to water. His network of "Uber" boats was set to carry Tino through the Caribbean Sea into the Gulf of Mexico.

He boarded his first fishing charter boat and sat back in route to the coast of Panama at latitude 9.638177 N; longitude -82.528603 bordering Costa Rica. Charter boat 1 dropped Tino off the side of the boat onto his Yamaha watercycle. He then rode his watercycle underwater from Panamanian waters into Costa Rica where Charter boat 2 awaited at latitude 14.956494 N; longitude -83.121593 W. Each charter had a fully charged battery pack to be flipped into the water scooter. In addition to this scooter maintenance, Tino checked coordinates and examined his route across these open waters. Now that he was in the midst of his open sea subway, Tino began to question the necessity of so many charter exchanges. *The Snowman* had a history of jumping from one boat to another as he smuggled drugs into the US. This new element of jumping one charter to another underwater was new, but to cover any trail of his escape, he wasn't going to spare any expense or effort at anonymity.

Charter boat 2 bypassed Nicaragua with a destination into Honduras. The charter cut through the ocean waters and anchored at the northern maritime border of Nicaragua latitude 14.951251 N; longitude -83.123549 W. Tino dropped the watercycle and once again, navigated underwater into Honduran waters. This time he arrived at eastern maritime border latitude 15.181351 N; longitude -83.153550 W in Honduras. After relaxing on the second charter boat and transitioning to scooter into the northern most Nicaraguan waters, the plan temporarily broke down.

Attempting to leave Nicaraguan territory on scooter trip number 2, Tino sped into some netting and got tangled alongside a huge haul of fish. The scooter propeller continued to churn away and tied Tino up in a huge section of the fish netting. Fortunately, after a few seconds of bouncing off fish and pulling in greater lengths of net, Tino regained composure and shut the scooter off. He hadn't planned how to free himself from a fishnet, but the nature of his business had prompted him to carry a huge, sharp knife to defend himself or dismember others, which ever came first. Crashing into a catch of fish churned a few into bloody chum in the water. Tino knew that he was turning in to a nice juicy bait for the nearest shark and he needed to act immediately to escape intact. He cut through the netting in short order and released a ton of fish in the process. He quickly shaved off lengths of netting cord to free his scooter. He could see some predator sharks taking notice of the haul of fish and the blood. Tino could feel a surge of adrenaline kick in. He holstered his knife and knew he needed to maintain calm to escape. Once free, he cranked the motor of his Yamaha without any response. Muttering to himself he worked through a checklist in his mind. Tino noticed a short length of rope from the net had locked up the propeller which prevented engine engagement. Becoming a little frantic with the shark closing in, he ripped the netting loose, fired up the scooter and made his next charter boat 10 minutes behind schedule. He had weathered enough violence that his nerves were pretty immune to the chaos he had encountered. Even with his experience, Tino couldn't believe in the vast open Caribbean waters that he would plow into a fishnet. Mental note – avoid schools of fish the rest of the trip.

Charter 3 connection then transported Tino to the Mexican Yucatan peninsula latitude 21.047198 N; longitude -86.642484 W. The short leg of underwater travel using his watercycle took him to latitude 21.592483; longitude -86.667189. The fishnet delay caused the next charter boat to pull up anchor and begin to move away from the coordinates. Tino was cruising along as planned on a beeline from the first boat off Honduras (which, as ordered, immediately headed to shore if Tino did not emerge in a given time window) toward the water boundary extending off the coast. This would have been disastrous in the open sea if it would have been necessary to track down the fishing boat.

His late connection to the Final charter outside Brownsville, Texas occurred about 35 minutes behind schedule since the delay with the netting compounded from one charter location to the next. His charter inside Mexican waters gave up when he was 25 minutes behind schedule. They had actually turned toward shore and had moved about 5 minutes from their designated gps location when Tino emerged from under water. After pulling himself onto the scooter and out of the water, he checked his longitude and latitude against a schedule. He knew to contact the missing boat. Prepared with a satellite phone in a waterproof pack strapped to his back, he set up office in the middle of the water. Tino contacted the charter and corrected their course for the pick-up.

The Snowman was making his way to the United States. A Mexican charter boat ferried him to within a half mile of the Brownsville, Texas border. From here he made the last scooter shuttle inside US maritime borders. This charter carried him the last length of the trip to a location outside Miramar Beach, Florida.

Once again, Tino donned his scuba suit and gear, launched the scooter with an extra battery pack, and sped toward the beach. His charter for the US landing had an extra assignment to provide for his transfer to land. During planning, Faustino had scoured the coastline on maps and a marina caught his eye for a first destination. Norriego Point was an unspectacular point on the map, but the namesake with his drug lord idol from Panama was too much of a sign. Such a small beach would seem to be a great landing spot for *The Snowman*. This landing would complete the water journey. The Gulf Coast connection had been directed to hide a dry set of clothing at the marina of this public beach.

After piloting the Scooter into Norriego Point Marina, Tino tripped an auto pilot device on the scooter to return the device to the last charter boat. This boat captain had been directed to retrieve and tow the scooter another three miles out to sea. The crew was to sink the water taxi and further minimize the chance of any evidence linking the trip to Tino. As a contingency, the charter was not to remain in the Gulf location more than two hours and while anchored at the gps site, everyone on board was to be fishing to carry out the masquerade.

The slight delays had pushed Tino's entry to Norriego Point an hour late and situated Tino and the scooter among a fleet of fishing boats returning from work. This seemed to serve Tino's favor as he cruised below water surface among the boats and used them as cover. Tino navigated to a marshy location at the beach and changed out the battery pack. The gps location was triggered on the scooter, he turned it around, walking in to a 5-foot depth of water, tripped the motor and shoved the unit off toward the Gulf waters. The unbelievable journey was successful, Tino turned and struggled onto land to strip off his wet suit and scuba gear. Tino was beside himself and let the euphoria of accomplishment take over his emotions, not looking back, Tino set up for the next phase of his relocation.

23

Identity Theft

He needed a new identity and preferably citizenship. His advance team had been staking out the beach and identified a local Latino construction worker the same build and similar in look to *The Snowman*. Tino had a name to call out and a highly predictable departure route for his target who completed his job and walked to his vehicle through the beach area like clockwork. Tino noticed this unsuspecting individual immediately. He had just made landing, slipped on some trunks and a beach shirt, and caught his prey within 10 minutes of shipping off the scooter. It was a tight schedule, but now things were falling into place to perfection. Tino called Martino's name, and the stranger spun around to see who had called for him.

Tino struck up conversation with Martino Randolsa and quickly made a connection. Within minutes, *The Snowman* made an invitation to drain a few Coronas. *The Snowman* sat with Martino at the **Hydration Station** on the coastal highway and got himself a bite to eat. The two exchanged backgrounds and soon chatted like long lost friends. Faustino carried on his charade until it was dark. Night darkness provided some cover to complete this phase of his "citizenship". Once he learned a few critical details to carry out this identity theft, he exited the bar with Martino and they worked their way toward and beyond the rear of the building and into the neighborhood. Martino turned to shake the hand of his new friend to say goodbye. Goodbye it was as *The Snowman* ran his right-hand past Martino's and jammed the scuba knife into Martino's stomach and pulled the weapon up and twisted the blade to inflict as much injury as possible. Simultaneous with the thrust of his knife, he covered Martino's mouth to stifle any screams and pushed him to the ground.

After watching Martino pocket his wallet, he knew right where to search to retrieve the identification and some pocket change to start the trip. Tino slit the man's throat to make sure he was dead and pulled him to a nearby commercial dumpster. He struggled to get the body into the fullest container. He wanted this body and the trash disposed of before the rank smell of a decomposing body would become noticeable. Faustino located some large empty boxes in the other two containers, retrieved them, broke them down to spread out and covered the body. Tino quickly left the site and worked his way to a predetermined storage facility arranged by one of his American drug dealers.

24

Like a Sore Thumb

Deliberate effort had been taken to eliminate any trail that would point the authorities in Tino's direction. Tino used contacts in his U.S. drug distribution chain of command to identify total strangers to buy cars, motorcycles, and pick-ups. His drug dealers were instructed to relocate from their community for one day to select locations in his escape itinerary. They were to carry no identifiable information, make no credit card purchases, and other than reaching out to beggars soliciting hand-outs, make no communication with people in each community. Once arriving in town, the local ***Buy and Sell*** newsletters were scoured for used vehicles to purchase. Once three vehicles were identified and confirmed by Tino's men as being available in a drive by of the locations, a panhandler was found to carry out the purchase. Panhandlers were given a $500 advance to make the contacts and close a purchase in addition to the cash asking price for the vehicle. A location was determined that the panhandler would bring the vehicle to and exchange the transport and keys for a $1000 fee to get lost and stay quiet. People as desperate as these beggars did not question anything once they received the $500. With a promise of another $1000 in cash, everyone solicited for the deal quickly fell in line. Most homeless people assumed that if the exchange location fell through, they had a vehicle to use or sell and $500 cash. Every one of the purchasers made good on a purchase and exchange to get the Total $1500 - a fortune in their minds.

The purchasers were instructed to offer the full asking price in cash to move things along. They signed their own name on the title page and turned that over with the vehicle. Documentation was burned beyond recognition after the panhandler had been driven away from the drop off. The first vehicle was placed in a closed storage facility arranged by the drug commander. The storage was locked with a mailed combination lock the purchasing agent carried with him. Not knowing when *The Snowman* was going to make his escape, care was taken to avoid an abandoned car or truck which might be investigated by the local authorities. Storing vehicles in a locked location removed the prospect of an investigation of abandoned cars or trucks. Suspicion was further removed by stashing the various transports in Mayberry RFD-like communities patrolled by Barney Fife deputies.

He activated the perimeter gate with the access code, made his way to building 3 and found the storage closet that had been rented. Tino quickly dialed the combination lock, tugged it open, and flicked the lock off the bracket. The door rolled up into the 8' by 12' unit to reveal a nondescript Honda motorcycle, a change of clothes, and a satchel with cash and some starter essentials such as razor, toothpaste, toothbrush, and deodorant. In order to start his trek and to gain details to enter the remaining garage facilities to exchange cars or trucks, *The Snowman* found the cell phone provided with the clothing and a charged, portable cellphone battery. In the lighted storage area, blood from the killing was readily visible on his clothes. Tino disrobed, changed into some of the clothing that had been provided, and worked through a checklist in his mind. Power up the cell phone with the portable battery, but do not turn the unit on. A map of his route was wrapped around the cell phone which he studied to get oriented. Then the storage room was emptied. Bloody clothing had to be disposed of. He double bagged the clothes, pulled the storage door down and took the lock. He mounted the Honda motorcycle and sped away into the night.

The bloody clothes were discarded in a gas station trash can he passed by. It was a clean get away. He pulled the cell phone up and texted "Check in". Tino raced his Honda bike up Florida Hwy 85 from Niceville, then to Crestview. Route 90 was picked up at Crestview which carried him 4 miles out of town to Milligan. Two miles before reaching Milligan, he found an open farm field, he pulled the bike to the side of the road and texted for additional information – "Whats next" was keyed into the phone. Upon arrival in Milligan, he stopped to check the phone for a message. Like clockwork, "front gate 172830* B 2 unit 59" was displayed. *The Snowman* backtracked his route out of town, torched the motorcycle and observed it burning in a swampy wooded area he noticed as he entered town. This particular road back to town was narrow and isolated. Only one car drove the flat road and Tino noticed it driving far enough away allowing him to slip into a wooded area and not be seen.

Tino hiked the remaining two miles into town and located the *Triple AAA Storage* in Milligan, Florida. This was a gated outside storage with a combination box for the 172830* code. An electric motor engaged pulling the front gate open on a track. Tino walked into the compound and looked for Building 2, then looked for unit 59 which was an exterior overhead garage door. *The Snowman* used the same combination code to unlock the combination and flipped it off the handle. He slid the handle out of the locking bracket and pulled the door up and open. This time he had a 4-year-old Ford Fiesta waiting for the next leg of the journey to Baker, Alabama. A new map sat on the driver seat marked with an orange marker to highlight the short route into Alabama and **EXTRA SPACE STORAGE** scratched across the bottom of the map. Three miles out of town he texted "What's next" and sat the phone in the passenger seat.

Once Tino used a transport to jump from one location to another, a hitchhiker would be picked up with an out of state hiking destination advertised on their hiking cardboard sign. "To New Orleans"….."To Houston"….."To Phoenix" although none really registered with Tino, he just hoped they were far away from where he was. Hitch hikers were offered the vehicles after a full tank fill up, money for a meal, and cash for an additional fill up.

Upon arrival at Baker, Tino pulled over to check the phone. Once again, a text was waiting, "front 0716# unit 33". Tino drove to an isolated truck stop nearby, topped off the tank with gas, and waited for someone looking for a ride. Not long after arriving and grabbing a can of Orange soda and some SlimJim sausage sticks to eat, he noticed a passenger jump from the passenger side of a semi and stride into the truck stop. Just as his lookouts had described, the young man carried a cardboard sign showing a destination.

The *Snowman* turned the car toward the road once he saw the hitchhiker setting up to start thumbing for a ride to "Beaumont, Texas" as defined by the cardboard sign. Tino drove away and once out of sight, he turned the car around and drove back toward the drifter. He took the suggestion of his planner and drove about 500 feet past the hiker before stopping. This was better than fishing! The young man jogged up to the car with the door open for his entry. Tino drove a half mile and made the pitch to give away the car. "I have a deal for you please" said Tino. "I don't need thees car anymore, would you like eet?" As suspicious as the hitchhiker was, the opportunity quickly won over his hesitation. With a look of disbelief on his face, the drifter rode with Tino to a building near **EXTRA SPACE STORAGE.** Tino exited the car with the engine running and handed the fellow some cash. The hitchhiker slipped the car into gear and drove away. "I deedn't like that Feeiesta anyway" Tino thought to himself.

How anyone could be traced through this maze was impossible

and that was the way Tino liked it. He walked toward the building to cover his intention in case the hitchhiker was paying any attention. After reaching the front of the building, *The Snowman* veered off toward the storage site. When he got to the gate, he noticed the security was a different type of lock. *The Snowman* wasn't familiar with this combination lock; a real estate type lock box which had to be opened to retrieve a key to the gate lock. Tino fumbled around with the 0716# code on the number cylinders and tugged at the lock. It wouldn't open the way he was used to. It would seem most likely to open at the yoke holding the box to the gate. Tino tried 0716# three times and got increasingly frustrated when nothing happened with the tug on the box. He finally stepped back in a rage and jammed the bottom of his boot against the box which jostled the base plate of the box open to reveal a key. Tino looked around to see if anyone saw him going postal on the little lock box. "Mr. Macho" finally calmed down and composed himself. After dropping the key in the dark, he found it and picked up the key. After inserting the key into the gate lock and sliding it from a bracket, he opened the gate.

Darkness had set in and identification numbers on the units were not easy to make out. In addition, the sequencing of the unit numbers followed no order. Fortunately, this was a small facility and knowing he needed an exterior door unit, he narrowed things down and found unit 33. This time Tino found a 2011 Nissan Rogue with a trunk of cash, more clothes, and two weapons. *The Snowman* found comfort by gripping the Pistol and eyeing an AK47 rifle. Ha Ha…. the drug cartel was back in business.

25

THE ADVENTURES OF MOVING

The series of vehicle flips created a ghost identification from one community to the next from Destin to *The Snowman*'s new Columbia….a small village in south Alabama. When Tino decided on his destination, he had been surfing maps on the Internet. All maps called for a destination to be entered into the app. A number of associates residing in the US suggested that *The Snowman* would be most comfortable in the mid-south to replicate the climate he was accustomed to in Columbia, South America. Reviewing maps helped him realize he liked the water bordering the mid-south. His options ranged from Texas to the Florida panhandle. Almost as if throwing darts at a wall, he pointed to Alabama. Out of familiarity, Tino decided to try Columbia and see if his country existed elsewhere.

At least in name he found a new Columbia. The details would be revealed upon arrival. After walking around Columbia for about an hour, he had virtually seen everything this village had to offer. Tino felt comfortable that no hazard existed for a full police force to swoop down on him. After all, only two uniformed police seemed to exist here. One officer worked from 6 a.m. until 3 p.m. while a second shift for policeman number two ran from 3 until midnight. No formal patrol occurred from midnight until 6 a.m. – this was the sleepy little village *The Snowman* had hoped to melt into when he initiated his escape.

Snowman logic was formulated in Columbia in a sparsely populated rural mountain area. Transportation was limited and communication was just as primitive. Tino assumed that a small rural community would be the best place to hide out. He chose his new Columbia based on his old Columbia. Yes, it was small. Yes, it was isolated. Yes, it was off the map. No, Tino did not blend in…not for a second…..not by a long shot.

The Snowman was new to this little town and clearly unrelated to anyone. "Hey boy, where you from?" Not "Hi", no "good morning", not even "how you doin?" "Hey boy, where you from?" was local code for you don't belong here and you better leave. The Barney Fife patrol immediately jumped into action and stopped Tino more than once a day to build an understanding of what the heck this guy was doing in our town. *Snowman* logic dictated marginal police force, marginal interaction. The reality was marginal police force, nothing better to do, might as well track this stranger with an electron microscope.

Tino was careful to stay out of sight and away from people, but the Motel 6 on the east side of town was the only lodging available and the clerks at the front desk might as well have run a tv news outlet from their work station. Every move he made was relayed to the officer on duty. If Tino went to the grocery, a patrolman was front and center. Barney I or Barney II did not matter, they were patrolling near the front entrance to every place Tino visited and were waiting for him upon exit. With only about 5 businesses in the small town to visit, their presence could have been a coincidence. Paranoia was setting in on Tino and he became convinced these cops were already looking for the famous escaped Snowman. These were not undercover cops either, these guys were so conspicuous that most people would have known this was small town policing. Not *The Snowman*, he felt like a hunted animal.

Where to go? Where to hide? Something had to change and quick. Tino couldn't take much more of this surveillance. He did notice almost everyone in town had some weird ritual of greeting one another. It had something to do with the color of sweatshirt or cap they had on. If someone had on orange and blue or had a word "AUBURN" on their clothes they would acknowledge one and other with "Wah Eaguhl". Tino could not understand "Wah Eaguhl", but he could tell Auburn had significance. Just as obvious was the connection he drew to other folks who liked the color red and shouted "Roh Tod" to one another. Most of these people had some swirly looking capital A on part of their clothing.

When orange bumped into red some inside joke was clearly known to everyone in town. "Wah Eaguhl" was treated like an obscenity if a red was greeted by an orange. Some red people would ignore the greeting and walk on staring blankly like no one said anything. Others would take issue and curse under their breath or occasionally bump into the orange person pretending it was an accident. If "Roh Tod" was shouted in the presence of orange, the same response occurred in reverse. Tino didn't understand these two gangs, but he made sure to keep red and orange out of his wardrobe. The cops were already making enough issue with him, he didn't need to accidentally trigger some gang warfare. He knew he could handle himself and wasn't afraid, but this small town was supposed to provide cover.

Tino frequented a small Mexican restaurant almost daily for one or even two meals. The options were almost nonexistent. The Mexican food was not Mexican, but it was closer to what he was used to than the competition. He tried **Geno's Burgers** and couldn't get over how greasy the food was. One trip and Geno was off the list. **Uncle Vic's** served what they referred to as "down home" food, but two trips to **Uncle Vic's** and Tino was experiencing gravy overload. **Tamala's Mexican Taco Shop** would be his go to. After about three days of double meals, he had broken the culture barrier with a waitress, Josette. There was no attraction to Josette - she was overweight which Tino did not like, he preferred his women on the anorexic side of extreme. She did not wear makeup to hide her natural appearance and always seemed to wear more food on her clothes than she delivered. But she was friendly.

Initially, Josette was waitress friendly and made small talk as part of the job. Fortunately for her, Tino was not accustomed to US currency and would leave pretty outlandish tips. A $10 tip on a $6 meal was a new experience for Josette, but she quickly got on the lookout for Tino and made sure to wait on his table whether it was her table or not.

Week 3 and Tino was about to go out of his mind. Police were everywhere he went. Not necessarily harassing him - but they harassed him. They did not venture into *Tamala's* to keep tabs on Tino, but they did hover outside the restaurant in their patrol cars while keeping an eye on the rest of the town. Inside *Tamala's*, Tino could interact without raising too much suspicion. Josette stopped at Tino's table as soon as she closed out an order. Tino asked if she could sit for a minute.

The Snowman was just dying to find out what this red and orange gang warfare was all about and how open the community was to allow such a blatant presence. Tino did his best to communicate his impression of the "culture" he encountered and better understand how to fit in to Columbia. He continued to describe the gangs he had made note of but with his heavy Latino accent needed to make about three attempts before things registered. Finally it registered on her and Josette laughed in his face long and hard - actually for about a half a minute…..not an eternity, but a long time to be laughed at when you're used to being feared. She talked with the presumption Tino knew all about Auburn University and The University of Alabama. He knew what a university was, but he didn't understand what THE universities were. It took a while to register but the color of team uniforms finally cleared up the underwhelming wardrobe selection among the town folk.

Josette didn't have time to spell out the history of team mascots (and probably didn't really know the truth) but she was pretty quick to enunciate "War Eagle" and "Roll Tide" clear enough for Tino to understand these were real words. Now he could check off a couple of boxes and better assemble his train of thought. *The Snowman* was so far off base with his initial choice of communities to blend in, but very slow to conclude how conspicuous he was in this little village. Over the next few days and trips to **Tamala's** Josette educated Tino on Alabama. He asked her for more information about the cities where these universities resided.

Once she described Auburn as a small-town community, Tino decided he would be about as conspicuous there as he was in this Columbia. Tuscaloosa, on the other hand, sounded big enough to fit into and small enough to lack the sophistication of a comprehensive law enforcement system. At least that was his interpretation and it sounded like a better choice than Columbia, Alabama.

26

Hank Returns to Scene of the Crime

Hank had very few mementos from his childhood or his family for that matter. One of his greatest treasures was a sleeve of photos taken at a photo booth when the family had visited Medellin on one of their "vacation" trips to the big city. A camera was not something the family had invested in since there was no place reasonably close to process the film. You have to keep in mind, Hank grew up in poverty as well as before smartphones were in everyone's pocket. Instead, his family portrait was a three-picture sleeve of the four of them crammed into a carnival photobooth to take the goofy girlfriend/boyfriend shots. Carlos clustered everyone in place and maintained a formal look among the four so that they had an occasional image to reflect on the growth and maturation of the kids. Unknown to any of them at the time, there would be one and only one sleeve of pictures taken. That sleeve had perched on the dresser in Carlos' and LaNita's bedroom for over a year.

Immediately following the attack on the home and murder of his family, Hank was sheltered in Seth and Lorraine's home. Early the next week, Seth had made the disgusting visit to the home to retrieve Hank's belongings and in his search, Seth saw the photos and knew it would be treasured. Seth stuffed bedding and clothes for Hank in a couple of pillowcases off the beds. They had bedding for Hank, but

Seth felt a need to find some keepsake items to give Hank a foothold on his past. Sitting front and center in the front room, knocked onto the floor, was a radio half wrapped in crumpled paper. Not realizing this assault interrupted a birthday party, Seth did not draw the connection of the radio to Hank. He took the radio and placed it in the car. Seth also took special care to sandwich the family portrait in a Bible in his car. It was a quick trip since he didn't want to spend time in this violent setting, plus, there was simply nothing more to collect.

As Seth retrieved the minimal amount of clothing and some medical supplies for Hank, he also took inventory of what was not available to bring home. Seth and Lorraine would need to sit and compile a shopping list to provide Hank with some standard possessions any normal child should have. Since Hank had virtually nothing, they started from scratch. The couple set about their task of providing for, but not overwhelming their new house guest. Both of these guardians became quite sad over the limited lifestyle Hank had considered normal.

Hank was reduced to tears when Seth took the picture from his Bible and presented it to him. *Thank you so much for this treasure. As much as I appreciate you and Lorraine, I need to think through my loss. Pictures of my family will help me deal with my pain,* thought Hank. When the radio was handed to Hank, he perked up just a bit. Life had been a whirlwind for Hank the last few days and he had nothing to relate to in his new home. At least now, he had a set of pictures to look at and reflect on as he processed his grief. With a little assistance from his foster parents, he would also have the entertainment of his own radio. Both treasures would be a reminder of his natural family and trigger some sadness. *If I could only talk with you about my hurt. I just do not understand any of this. Why did they do this to my family?*

Hank had secured a broken plastic mop handle for a pointing

stick at his home in El Ocaso. There was really no reason for Seth to see his pointer tool as anything more than broken trash, but this had purpose for Hank, and he wanted his pointer. Now that he had the family pictures, Hank had an image to personalize his communications. The missing link was the set of cards that he and Carmelita had arrived at for Hank to provide some input into his activity. *Where are my cards? Seth knew to get the picture; would he get the cards?*

Hank had the pillowcase with his outfits and a blankie he related to since he was an infant. The second pillowcase was sitting on the floor nearby, but he was immobile and could not navigate to his other "worldly goods". Seth was out of the house, but Lorraine was in the other room and Hank needed her attention. He began to bang his hand on the table where they had placed him. *I will signal for attention just like I did with Carmelita,* as he slammed his hand to the tabletop 3 times, then paused, then 3 slams, then pause over and over until Carmi showed up. Four rounds of pounding and finally Lorraine provided some attention.

"Hey, hey buddy, do you need something?" Lorraine asked as she entered the room. She strode over to the table where Hank sat pointing toward the case on the floor. He raised his hand then glided it toward the pillowcase. "Hmmm, you want me to move your arms?" as Lorraine allowed guess number 1.

Oh geeeezzz, Hank thought, *only 63 more questions to go. I have all day if Lorraine will stay with me.* Hank rocked back in his chair and started the side to side "No" gesture. Once again, he moved his hand from the table toward the floor. The movement was somewhat spastic, but it was a motion toward the only thing nearby.

"You want the pillowcase?" asked Lorraine.

Hank mustered the best smile of affirmation he could and began his back and forward "Yes" gesture. Lorraine grabbed the pillowcase and emptied the contents onto the table. *Dang, quick learn,* thought Hank.

Lorraine patted him on the back and eyed a Liberty Bell in a small scaffold that they brought with them from the States. "If you need anything, ring this bell", Lorraine said as she poked the bell and made it ring. "Can you do that?"

Hank swung at the bell and rang it but knocked it over. *Good try Ms. Lorraine, but I don't know if that is gonna work.*

Lorraine got some tape and anchored the bell frame to the table to stabilize the bell for Hank.

Hank was halfway paying attention when he spied the small ring of communication cards he and Carmelita had used. He inched his arm toward the ring as steady as he could and finally trapped a piece under his hand. Hank pawed the ring toward him. He finally situated the ring in front of him and popped the ring with his hand. *Please work with me and the cards, please?* Hank thought toward Lorraine. He had the most pathetic look on his face, but it must have done the trick.

"So this is special, huh?" Lorraine said. "You want to show them to me?"

Hank fiddled with the cards the best he could, then stopped at the YES card.

"Oh, you do want to show me" Lorraine chimed in.

His card selection was limited, after all, it was a creation by Carmelita and Hank and neither one was older than 12. Hank pulled the cards apart and found the BED card. He pointed to it hoping to explain himself to Lorraine. He was trying to say HOME but that just wasn't in the radar of the brother and sister since they were always there.

"Are you tired?" asked Lorraine.

Hank fumbled through and found the NO card. He slid the card on the ring toward Lorraine.

"Hmmm, not tired but bed". She thought out loud. "So you want your blankie?"

NO card. Then Hank had a thought. He put the BED card next to the family picture sleeve.

"Hank, they are gone. You cannot sleep with them." Lorraine voiced.

Come on, work with me here. Hank was visibly frustrated when he slid another card into view. OUTSIDE.

"BED, Family, OUTSIDE….. BED, Family, OUTSIDE….. BED, Family, OUTSIDE….." Lorraine thought through the sequence while speaking it quietly to herself.

Hank's hand and arm gestures were simply too wild to have meaning for someone that was not intimately familiar with him. That did not stop him from attempting to gesture outside thinking *GO* ! He beat his chest with his hand once, dropped to the OUTSIDE card, moved to the Family pictures, then rested his hand on the BED card. *C'mon - take me outside and go to where my family bed is !!!* Hank was really frustrated.

"Hold on Hank, I will figure this out. Don't get upset." Lorraine said reassuringly. "You want something…..it has to do with your family…..duh, duh, duh….OUTSIDE BED." She repeated her thoughts again. "This has to do with your family" she said.

Hank poked at the YES card.

"Is there a bed outside?" she asked.

You have to be kidding, he thought as he poked NO. His eyes were close to rolling out of their sockets.

"It's really not about the bed is it?" Lorraine asked. "Is it where the bed is?"

Hank poked YES.

"You want to go outside to go to your home" Lorraine spoke with some conviction.

Hank poked YES. *She is so much smarter than Seth.*

"Seth, we need to make another trip to El Ocaso for Hank. He needs to look for something." Lorraine explained.

"Seriously, there was nothing at the house of any value at all" Seth responded. "You sure that is what he wants?"

"I have been through a good interaction with him with labeled cards from his pillowcase. No doubt in my mind and he is pretty emphatic."

This time, all three of them made the trip and Lorraine brought the ring of labeled cards. Thirty minutes of driving gave Lorraine an opportunity to try to determine what Hank needed from the house. They were both concerned about him returning to the scene of the devastation, but they wanted to help him process things any way they could. At least they would be with him to wheel Hank out of the house if he began to have a reaction. Lorraine's card interrogation went nowhere since the communication selection was so limited. They pulled up to the house, sat for a moment in the car facing the front door while Seth offered a prayer for Hank's family and for Hank dealing with the entire ordeal.

27

Hidden Treasure

Hank wanted his pointer stick since it extended his capacity to identify objects and people. Just because he did not see anything similar in the short time he had been with the Grissoms, he was not aware that something nicer could have been bought or made to suit his needs. *I really am better at getting what I need when I can point further. I really didn't have any way to share that with Lorraine, and not being able to wheel myself, it is just something I need.*

Seth pulled the sling stroller out of the car and then picked Hank up and placed him in the seat. They rolled up the rickety ramp with Lorraine bringing up the rear. No one felt comfortable with entering the house, particularly with the dried puddles of blood and the lingering odor of stale air. Hank attempted to signal the direction into his bedroom he had shared with Carmelita. Once inside his room, he surveyed until he found the stick he was looking for. One dresser that Carlos had made for their clothes was in the room with two small beds that they had used. He gradually got Seth to push him to the location of the stick, but it remained out of his reach. Seth and Lorraine took turns touching objects that would give Hank something to react to - but a broken mop stick did not register on them and they both passed over it. *How could you get so close and not* see my stick? You're driving me crazy !....then he arched his back in the stroller as Lorraine made a second pass over the stick to get her attention.

"You're kidding me. This stick is what you want?" she asked.

Hank began sorting for the YES card when Lorraine handed him the stick. He reached for the stick and grabbed it and her hand with his lower arm and pulled it to his head. He had the stick, but he also was so thankful for Lorraine's intuition. He just held her hand against his head and began to trickle some tears. I don't know how I will make it without you. Thank you.

Lorraine noticed the tears on his cheeks as they began to drop against her skin. She reached under Hank's chin and pulled it up so their eyes would meet. "Don't you worry Hank; we will figure this out. Just be patient with us as we will be with you. Is there anything else we need to pick up?"

Hank swung the stick toward the bedroom doorway. Seth wheeled him into the front room where Hank swung the stick to the side room. I need to see what Papi' was hiding in that room. I just need to know.

Seth wheeled him into the side room. Hank used his stick and began poking different planks in the floor. Click, click, click, click, clonk, click. He tapped the stick across the floor and heard the clonk, hollow sound, then got a click on the next plank. Oh boy, how am I going to get Seth to buy into this and get under that floor? He made another pass over the planks but continued tapping the hollow plank repeatedly when he got on the target plank. Click, clonk, clonk, clonk, click….as he moved onto and off the target.

"Do you know something about the floor?" asked Seth. "Let me take a look." As he knelt down to examine the flooring. Seth began knocking on the floor with his knuckles and was convinced the single plank had a different tone. "I am going to get some tools from the car." Seth worked his way off the floor and strode out to the car.

He returned with a toolkit and dropped back to the floor. Seth pulled a flat blade screwdriver from his tools and looked for an opening to wedge the tip between planks. Finally, he retrieved a hammer to tap the screwdriver into the edge of the plank to get a better position to pry the flooring loose. Looking around, he saw just how dilapidated the house was and abandoned any concern to preserve the flooring.

Seth finally loosened the plank and lifted it out of place to reveal the cavity between the floor foundation. Upon first look, the white pvc pipes looked like the plumbing for the bathroom and kitchen sink. When Seth reached between the floor joists, he was able to grip the pipe which he intended to shake to see how firm it was connected to the plumbing network. Instead, a section approximately 18" long lifted easily out of the cavity.

Once he had lifted the pipe, he noticed that both ends of the section were capped with a threaded pvc cap. Seth twisted against the pipe and one cap gradually let loose. As the cap was removed, Seth was shocked with what he found inside. Some currency was showing immediately. He dug into the contents and pulled out paper money as well as some paperwork. The papers were neatly folded and tucked into separate envelopes.

Hank and Lorraine could see that some currency was covering the contents of the pipe and their curiosity shot through the ceiling. *Papi', what have you done for me Papi'?* Seth opened the first envelope on the top. Inside was a life insurance policy with a $100,000 premium. This document listed each member of the family as a beneficiary, LaNita showed as the primary for 100% recovery. The kids were listed as secondary beneficiaries if they survived LaNita. Carmelita and Hendrick were assigned $50,000 each with the other sibling serving as an alternate beneficiary in the event of loss of life.

Seth pulled more policies from the envelope. One policy was made out against Carlos' life for Carmelita as the primary for $100,000. Her policy listed Hendrick as a secondary beneficiary followed by LaNita as a third beneficiary. Another policy identical to Carmelita's was made out for Hendrick as a primary, then Carmelita, then LaNita as survivor order.

Seth pulled a flashlight from his toolkit and examined the floor cavity further. As far as the beam from the light could shine, he did not see any additional pipes or other canisters. He was convinced the single pvc length was the extent of Carlos' buried treasure. Just from the cash value of the policies, it was an unbelievable find for Hank's benefit. "I do not see anything else for us to review from under the floor. Let's go outside and get some fresh air and see what else remains for examination." For no understandable reason, Seth set the plank back in place and stomped it back into position.

He tucked the pvc unit under his arm and wheeled Hank out the front door and down the ramp. Lorraine carried all the papers from the discovery. The threesome rolled up to the front passenger door of the car and Lorraine sat facing Hank and Seth behind them. Two unopened envelopes remained. One was not labeled and contained birth certificates, marriage certificates, and Columbian registry of identification. Carlos had really gone out of his way in provision for his family in the event things went sour. The policies were significant enough, but he had also thought to include all the necessary identification to associate with a death certificate if the family needed to exercise the insurance. How anyone was supposed to be aware of the find under the flooring was another issue, but things had worked out. Consummate family man, that was Carlos.

The final envelope was marked with each year beginning with 2001 followed below one year to another until the current year of 2011. Inside this envelope were clusters of money bills fastened together by rubber bands. Each year, Carlos had put away the equivalent of $500 a month ($6,000 a year) with the exception of year 2001 when he had begun his second job. During 2001, his concern was to pay off medical expenses, but he still decided to put away $200 a month just in case the worst happened immediately. All in all, Carlos had stashed $62,400 in cash to help out his family. Seth and Lorraine were purely awestruck with the find. They were not at all thinking about themselves, but they realized that Hank was instantly one of the wealthier people in a small town like La Quiebra.

Carlos was wise to conceal any evidence of accumulated wealth while serving within the drug chain. People would begin to speculate on any signs of an income shift while only working as a laborer in a mine. While he never believed it would come to pass, Carlos wanted some assurance the family was taken care of if he were killed. His hope had been a relocation and to utilize the savings he had set away under the floor. Carlos never stopped to count it, he just knew what he could save and he did that every month for years.

Hank didn't have a voice to use and Seth and Lorraine had suddenly lost theirs. They just sat for a few minutes contemplating what was in store. Finally, Seth broke the ice. "Hank, I am not sure you understand what all the papers and money amount to that we just found……that YOU just found. Hank, you are able to do pretty much whatever you want for the foreseeable future. We will help you process things and help you plan. Your Dad did a wonderful thing, even though he took a terrible risk in the process."

Lorraine piped into the conversation, "This is a lot of money and very important papers that we probably need to place somewhere for the immediate time. I suggest we head to Medellin to rent a deposit box for Hank and store his valuables." It was a weekday and midafternoon, so they did have time to make the stop. "Hank, can you handle a little more travel?"

Hank was clutching his communication ring and found the YES card. After displaying that as the most prominent card, he realized he was exhausted. He slumped back in his stroller almost lifeless. Seth picked him up and situated him in the car seat, packed up the stroller, and the two adults climbed in the car and backed away.

Within a minute, Lorraine peered into the back seat and found Hank sleeping a very deep sleep.

Before they knew it, Seth had the car parked in front of the bank they used for their accounts. He retrieved a briefcase with some room to spare to contain Hank's policies and money, stuffed the documents inside, then left the car to enter the bank. A service teller greeted Seth and asked about the church. After a quick exchange of greetings, Seth completed the paperwork and signed on behalf of Hank. He was escorted into a steel bar vault which contained walls of lock boxes which were double keyed. Access required the bank master key and the renter's key. Hank's box was located, keyed open, the box removed and placed on a chest high table. The service teller left Seth to make his box entry. Shortly after depositing Hank's documents, Seth slid the box into the vacant slot, flipped the door shut, turned his key to lock it in place and left the vault.

Seth could now turn his attention to processing the insurance policies. Sadly, he pulled together the death certificates for each of the family members who had been murdered and contacted the agent from the insurance company. The wheels turned a little slower than expected, but over the course of the next six months, another $300,000 was paid out to Hank and placed in the bank account in Medellin. He was the primary on one account for $100,000 and in succession, rose to the beneficiary on identical face value policies for LaNita and again for Carmelita. In total, Hank had just under $375 thousand dollars working for him in the bank.

Seth had managed to secure and safely make the deposit of all the funds into an account for Hank. Seth or Lorraine were co-signatures on any withdrawal that had Hank's mark. Hank could not sign documents, but he could make a crude "X" in the presence of a bank officer that would serve as his authorization. Working within the church, neither Seth nor Lorraine had ever dealt with or imagined managing that sum of money, so Seth took it upon himself to talk with some local brokers to determine a relatively safe, but more lucrative means of investing the funds than a standard bank savings account. In fact, as the various deposits were made, the tellers were awestruck with the denominations deposited. It was not every day $62,400 in cash and $300,000 in a cashier check would roll into an account.

Some people may have made a little more fanfare when processing these amounts of money, but Hank really had not grasped the significance of his wealth. Seth didn't really have any attachment to the investments other than as a guardian for Hank. Mind you, there are guardians in the world that would have sticky fingers in a situation such as this. Seth and Lorraine were unphased by the money and the circumstance. They understood what Hank had gone through and only wanted what was best for him.

28

Point of No Return

Unknown to Tino, part of the plan had broken down.....when he landed at Destin with the Yamaha water scooter, he activated an autopilot device to return the scooter unmanned to the last charter. Once he triggered the autopilot, he watched the slight bubbling of the propeller rippling across the water surface. Seeing the unit navigate about 200 yards, Tino left the water and began his land-based journey. *The Snowman* didn't see the ripples veering into the starboard side of a fishing boat approaching the docks to moor at a pier and unload their catch. When the scooter bumped into the fishing boat it veered into a clump of sea grass and tangled up. Within minutes, the scooter had gotten so entangled, there was no way it would self-correct in order to make the return to the charter. As was predetermined, the charter captain pretended to continue a fishing excursion for the next 3 hours awaiting the return of the unmanned scooter. In order to minimize any suspicion, the charter pulled up anchor and left the bay.

The charter made way to port at Panama City Beach for the rest of the afternoon. Charter captain fueled the boat, made way into the marina for a bite to eat, then returned to his boat. As dusk set over the Gulf of Mexico, the captain pulled his vessel away from the marina and cut back across the Gulf to Port Arthur, Texas hoping that the indirect navigation would distract anyone that may have noticed the "fishing" end of the trip offshore at Destin. No communication, no stops requested by Coast Guard, no concerns that the special passenger had been on board. Wouldn't have made much difference since the passenger had boarded in the middle of the Gulf, made limited communication, had not shared any name or identification, and paid a handsome amount of money to keep things that way.

Meanwhile, the scooter had been churning away in the sea grass, breaking apart shoots of the vegetation, and basically building a highly visible nest for the scooter to rest on. Not 24 hours had passed when the scooter was found and reported to the local authorities. Destin Police Department officers were used to some abandoned watercraft, but this was the first time a water scooter had been scuttled. This looked like a pretty expensive piece of diving equipment and other than the tangled seaweed and grasses, seemed to be brand new. The scooter was pulled from the grass and hauled into the precinct building and filed for missing equipment. The unit carried a vehicle number and serial number in addition to the model and manufacturer. The lost scooter was logged into the precinct data base which automatically associated the unit with a national CrimeStopper registry. Surely the owner would come looking for this device in short order.

A week later, with no contact regarding the scooter, an officer assigned to recovered equipment and vehicles activated the database to trigger exploration within the federal network. This was not the typical equipment associated with crime, but a review was standard operating procedure and you never knew where an investigation would take you.

29

Water Scooter Investigation

Information on the water scooter churned in the federal data base for over a month. This water craft was of interest more for its novelty than for any evident link to a crime. Nonetheless, Cy Reeder of the Houston Branch of the Federal Bureau of Investigation picked up the trail and took particular note that a water scooter with this identification was purchased in the past year, but from a dealer in Turbo, Columbia. What was a sea scooter from Turbo, Columbia doing on the shores of Destin, Florida? Cy was more curious than suspicious and decided to step up his review.

A quick call from Cy to the dealer of sale in Macon, Georgia yielded no direct linkage to *The Snowman* or anyone else for that matter. Mitch had been with **Divers Supply** on Mercer University Drive for the past 8 years. He wasn't certain how it had occurred, but the records of transaction showed the vehicle ID and related identification, but the purchaser had been redacted from his records. Until this investigation, the dealer wasn't even aware the equipment had been sold from his company. This was pretty peculiar since the accounting for the dealership had cleared a couple of years of audits. Then again, the auditor was balancing sales against receipts and as long as the numbers held up, names were simply out of the equation. As a peripheral offering, the dealer did note that three other scooters had been purchased the previous two years by one person for delivery to Cartagena, Columbia, South America. The dealer quickly located the Cartagena shop and contact information he had on hand. While he was comfortable he had done nothing wrong, he wanted to appease the FBI. He had watched enough tv to realize he did not want to be in the crosshairs of the FBI and he wanted them off his back.

Lisa took the call at **Diving Planet** in Cartagena, Colombia. She heard the name Cy Reeder, but his reference to the Federal Bureau of Investigation did not register with Lisa. Lisa was in a small city in Columbia and "Federal Bureau of Investigation" was just a foreign language to her. She didn't question the nature of the call. **Diving Planet** was a hub for diving expeditions and its location on the coast in the tropical climate resulted in communications from all over the Americas. In addition, **Diving Planet** had developed quite a distribution business for all kinds of scuba gear. A quick scan of her computer data base was all it took to pull up the receipt and delivery of the Yamaha Li sea scooters. Their records showed a scanned and signed authorization invoice showing the acquisition of the scooters, one device on each of four occasions over a two-year time frame. While there was no physical address for the recipient and the signature was scribbled beyond any recognition or readability, the phone number to contact the purchaser was available. Area code and prefix for the calls were consistent from one pick up to another, but the trailing four digits of each call was unique. Lisa did not pick up on any pattern, but Cy was in investigation mode and his inner Sherlock Holmes was in full gear. Following a little small talk from Cy to determine if Lisa would be any more of a resource, he thanked her for the info and hung up.

Not long after talking with Lisa, Cy was able to determine that these were burner phones, but all were assigned a call number for the same geographic area. He realized that he would not gain any communication information from burner phones, and without the phones, no purchasing information on the units could be obtained. Now Cy was more curious than before with the circumstances, despite having proportionately less information to digest. No conclusion jumped off the page. Cy needed to look at more pages. The area code and lead prefixes did help him determine that the hub of the communications with **Diving Planet** had to originate in Medellin. Now he had a location and timeframe but wasn't sure it had anything to do with any crime. An open-ended set of circumstances only fueled Cy's resolve to figure out the mystery.

30

Connect the Dots

His investigation now shifted from activity in and around Destin, Florida to reports of criminal activity associated with Medellin. Cy made contact with the Policia in Medellin. Cy's uneducated impression of Medellin allowed him to falsely conclude he would be dealing with a primitive law enforcement agency. In very quick fashion, Cy changed his perception of the community and the people. He had expected slow or no response from a back woods uneducated patrolman. Not only was he surprised with the fluent interaction with an English-speaking officer, Cy was blown away with the sophistication and resource he had stumbled upon. His contact on the phone was Sebastian and he was an amazing resource.

All Cy knew of the area was that Pablo Escobar had run his drug cartel out of Medellin in the 1980's and that crime was rampant. Years had passed and so had Escobar. The municipality had cleaned up significantly and the local government was noted for effective and efficient oversight and development.

Sebastian immediately synched up with Cy to patch together the information shared and ran incident reports under the parameters of the dates Cy provided. Only a few circumstances pulled up as open reports. Sebastian reviewed a few cases that may warrant Cy's attention. One of the most intriguing was a violent crime against a family murdered in a remote area outside of Medellin. According to the report, this family of four from El Ocaso had been brutally tortured and three of the family murdered. The fourth person, a little boy with physical disabilities had been left abandoned on site to fend for himself. An anonymous tip had been called in weeks after the attack and implicated a drug operation that preyed on the rural locals. The tipster attributed the attack to Faustino and Raul Carmona. Evidence of the drug operation continued from the attack until the tip when the authorities began the hunt for the two Carmona brothers. Occasional sightings of Raul were noted, but Faustino had disappeared from the countryside with no evidence of his existence. No reports of Raul had been received in over a year. Faustino had become a ghost for over two years.

Sebastian reviewed the case in great detail with Cy. The entire authority of Columbia had been devastated by the reports surrounding the case. Of particular concern was the gruesome profile of the attack on the three deceased. National attention had been devoted to this case largely because the killers were extremely violent with the nature of the murders, but also left a traumatized little boy alive, but alone and unable to talk or move. Fortunately, the authorities found the child shortly after the attack was completed. People shuddered at the thought of this little boy with cerebral palsy knocked from his chair and unable to help himself. To make matters worse, it was evident he had witnessed the entire scene and could not help the investigators with any descriptions or even intelligently respond to questions.

Sebastian was able to report that at least the boy had been taken in by a husband and wife from a church missionary in the area. To the officer's knowledge, the couple had adopted the boy and took him with them upon return to the United States. Sebastian was able to share the couple's name, the Grissoms, and their affiliation with the Arisen Son Church in Tuscaloosa, Alabama. As far as the Carmona brothers, little could be reported as to their whereabouts, let alone if they still existed. Their home and operations center had been found and staked out for the past two years. Everyone and anyone associated with the drug operations had scattered and attempts to follow up always ended without conclusion. People were clearly in total fear of retaliation based on the mythical stories of torture and murder associated with the Carmonas. If anyone knew anything, they were not going to share. Fear for self was one thing, but everyone knew that tracing reviews to any confidant was to jeopardize entire families. Sebastian offered to stay in touch if anything surfaced, but this case was the biggest puzzle for all officers in his department and he held no hope to close this event.

31

Hank Talk

Small steps were required, at least for Seth and Lorraine, to establish a communication system with Hank. Initially, Seth felt like Hank needed to understand "Yes" and "No" so he could engage in another version of 64 questions. First questions had to do with narrowing a category of interest or need to Hank. Well, that was Seth's take on the process.

I can't believe we are starting this all over again, **thought Hank.** *It took me long enough to train Carmelita when I had to go to the bathroom and when I was hungry. I will try to make this as painless as possible. He has these cards with a smiley face and a frowny face. Smiley has Y-e-s under the face. Frowny has N-o below. I like things that make me smile and don't want things that make me frown. Seth acts like a puppet for me and does this routine of excitement and saying "Yes, Yes, Yes" and pats my hand. If I could, I would bark for him since he makes me feel like a puppy. I have to admit, the Frowny means "No, not interested", to me, but puppet man gets excited and smiles as he says "No, No, No". I am confused...why does Seth smile for the Frowny card. I get "No", but why the smile.*

Seth then says, "Are you thirsty?", takes Hank's hand, taps his hand on the Yes Smiley card, and produces a glass of water. Seth takes a drink from the cup through a straw, sets it down, and says "Thirsty" and smiles.

So Seth asks me if <u>I am thirsty</u>, he takes a drink, then he is happy. I wonder how I am supposed to know Seth is thirsty? This is awkward.

Then Seth says, "Are you tired?" and pauses for a few seconds. Suddenly, Seth pulls up a pillow and lays his head on it, then he says, "tired, are you tired?" and pulls Hank's hand to the Frowny, No card, and smiles. "Are you tired?"

Now Seth asks me if <u>I am tired</u>, lays his head on a pillow, then he smiles. I wonder how I am supposed to know Seth is tired? This is really awkward.

Hank decides to take things in his own hands. He raises his hand and plops it on the pillow. Then Hank separates the cards which Seth placed one on the other. Hank swings his arm to the Frowny card. He pauses.

Now Hank bumps the glass of water with his hand and sloshes a little on the table. Once again, Hank swings his arm to the Frowny card. He pauses. Seth looks at Hank intently.

Then Seth announces, "You are not tired!" "You are not thirsty!"

Then Seth asks, "Are you thirsty?" and waits for a second. Then he points and says simultaneously, "Yes" pointing to Smiley, and "No" pointing to Frowny. Seth repeats, "Are you thirsty?" and pauses.

Hank waves to the Frowny card and rests his hand on it now that he has it separated.

Seth says, "No, you are not thirsty?"

Hank hesitates, then answers the question with a wave and resting his hand at *"Yes" I am not thirsty*.

Seth says, "Oh, you are thirsty!"

Hank doesn't hesitate, then answers the question with a wave and resting his hand at *"No" I am not thirsty*. In addition, Hank does an eye roll. For all his limitations, Hank can roll his eyes.

Seth says, "OH, you are not thirsty!" Hank wanted so badly to give him a thumbs up, but his motor response was not there. Instead, Hank gives Seth a smile of agreement – not a toothy smile, more of a smirky smile. Then Seth retorts, "You are not thirsty!"

Hank spastically places his hand on the pillow. Then he waves it toward the Frowny card and lands his hand on NO.

Seth announces, "You are not tired!" "You are not tired!"

Hank smirks the smile and thinks to himself, I think Seth has been taught the meaning of Yes and No.

Seth completes the lesson by hugging Hank and saying "Good boy, you are a smart boy".

Hank just seethes to himself, Go ahead, treat me like a dog, just know, I taught you, not the other way around.

This type of dialogue went back and forth for days as Seth would introduce more objects, more activities, more needs – each with a new picture card and new symbols underneath the picture. In Seth's mind, Hank was a quick read and seemed to actually be smart to a certain degree.

In Hank's mind, Seth is a quick read and pretty smart!

Lorraine would join in and she was very intuitive. Lorraine would come up with combinations of cards that Hank could Yes or No. Lorraine would encourage Hank with an "I just love it when we can share ideas!" or "You are so fine, I can't believe I thought this would be hard for us." Lorraine really developed the vocabulary and complexity of this card system. Hank was encouraged that Lorraine was so considerate and acknowledged him as a partner in this process. Lorraine was a wonderful person and really knew how to consider his needs, but more important, his feelings.

Lorraine really gets it, **Hank thought.**

I'll just keep working on Seth, maybe he will pick up on this communication deal soon..... SIGH! **thought Hank.**

32

The Marvel of T.V.

Hank adapted to the challenge of teaching Seth and Lorraine how to communicate with him. Interacting with more than one person in a systematic process was a huge step forward for Hank, but the big impact that caught Hank's attention was the television. Again, put yourself in Hank's shoes and think what a novelty a t.v. would be. He was in no way used to such a variety of programming. Growing up with his family, they did not have television as an option. On occasion, the family would pile into the rickety old truck and drive into Medellin for a movie. Those events were the equivalent of what most would consider an annual vacation away from home. Hank's vacation history was one day a year. Those single days carried Hank and the family from one year to the next.

After the attack that took his family and Hank had been taken into Seth and Lorraine's home, many new opportunities were revealed. Representing a church missionary, very little expense was budgeted for frills, but living in the U.S., the Grissoms did not consider television a frill – it was part of the fabric of their lives. Once he became a member of the Grissom household, Hank became aware of the presence of television. Missionary budget television amounted to what could be picked up from an over air antenna. Medellin had a lot to offer in tv broadcasting, but Seth's mission field was on the outskirts of Medellin and only two stations could be received. What was a disappointment for Seth and Lorraine was a marvel to Hank.

Regardless of how limited the broadcast content was, every program was a treasure of knowledge for Hank. He soaked up everything like a sponge and started to develop a much broader knowledge of life and the many possibilities people had. Hank did not comprehend the distinction between fact and fiction, but he understood everything he viewed.

Carmelita had provided Hank with more than she knew through her interaction and caring practices. He had the necessary ingredient of stimulation for his brain and as a result of the misperception of his family and limited visitation from neighbors, he processed any and everything he was exposed to in his infant and toddler years. His brain was fully developed compared to peers and advanced in some areas, but without speech, no one knew his ability. Despite the frustration of being misunderstood, underestimated, and often times neglected, Hank made the most of every interaction and the presence of communications among his family. How often did Hank sit in his chair, often slumped over, and be talked about by his family while present, but disengaged......"*Hello, I am right here, you are talking about me! Why do you not talk to me? I can't believe you said that about me as if I cannot hear.*" What Hank would give to be ignored by his family again. Now he was living with relatively unknown adults who were showing significant investment in him, he was developing a universally useful communication ability, and this crazy thing called television was going to rock his world.

33

Planting a Family

Lorraine and Seth did not take long to realize they would formally adopt Hank. Seth worked through the Medellin government to fulfill all requirements of adoption. Compared to the process in the United States, this was a pretty straightforward event. In addition to a culture of helping and caring that was evident throughout this government, the severity of Hank's involvement and the Grissom's interest and willingness to parent him smoothed the formality of this process. He would never get over what he witnessed of his family being mercilessly slaughtered, but Hank understood that he needed to move on. The resources and care these new parents provided went a long way in Hank's adjustment. As Hank became more adept with the communication system, he was able to have a little more command over his day. Lorraine came up with a method of placing similar cards of meaning on a common key ring. She even came up with the idea of color-coding groups of cards with common meanings, values, or activities. With familiarity in use of the system, even Seth was able to expand the capacity of the system and grow Hank's expressive vocabulary. What started out as a 64 Questions yes/no exercise was a legitimate way for Hank to improve his quality of life. He did not get everything he asked for, but just the opportunity to ask was a huge improvement in how Hank felt about himself.

I sure do miss Mami' and Pape' and Carmelita. Hank tried not to think of them too often, but he did flashback often and quickly have tears in his eyes. He had become much more attuned to his emotions from all the tragedy. That was such a low point in his life, but Hank was thankful for the Grissoms showing interest and caring for him. They provided much more for him than he ever experienced before. But he would trade it all for his family back with him and taking care of him.

Lorraine and Seth sat down with Hank one evening after a nice meal. They were all managing to be more conversant with one another in their own way. This was starting to feel like it should be something. Hank had no concept of getting married, he was too young, but when Lorraine said, "we have something very important to discuss with you" Hank began to get a really great, warm feeling inside. The anticipation was very real, but Hank did not really get what was coming next. Seth took over, "Hank, we are so sorry for what happened to Carlos and LaNita and your sister Carmelita. That hurts us as well as you, and we can't feel as you do about that terrible action. We do love you Hank, we care for you, and we want to take care of you."

All that was missing was in sickness and in health, etc.

"Hank, we want you to be a part of our family. We would like to adopt you and be your new mother and father. What do you think about being our son?"

What do I think about being your son......Oh my God – I did not know this was possible. You have taken me in, you deal with my limitations and struggles, you even try to understand me. Where do I sign up!!

Hank was overcome with emotion. Where was a smiley card when you needed one? This felt like he was thinking about his real family and a tear was welling up in his eye. Such a good tear this was. In the absence of a Smiley face, Hank leaned toward Lorraine and Seth and with all the control he could muster, swung his arms forward. "As parents do" Lorraine and Seth knew to lean into Hank. Somehow, the threesome managed to melt into a unit with the best group hug known to man. Hank was on top of the world. *Kumbaya!!!*

34

Relocation

Seth, Lorraine, and Hank began the arduous task of packing to move from one country to another. Their belongings were quite meager compared to what most people in the United States assemble in five years. Nonetheless, packing had to be compact and efficient for shipping. The car used by the Grissoms was provided by Arisen Son International and stayed behind with the team of clergy who now were on their own. As the five-year mission was completing, some sad good-byes were exchanged among the members of the church. Hank was struggling to comprehend what was happening. After the attack in his home at El Ocaso, the move to La Quiebra was beyond his comprehension. When Seth tried to describe their pending relocation to the United States, Hank just sat blankly with little to say. "I know what you mean when you talk about El Ocaso. I understand that La Quiebra is different from El Ocaso. But you talk about United States and I have no idea what that "city" is. Why are we leaving? You mentioned that your work in Columbia was done, but what does "done" mean? I really have no idea what is going on. I do appreciate what you and Lorraine are doing for me as new parents, I really do. I have never had such a nice home, such fresh clothes, and different types of delicious food. But I want my Papi' and Mami' and Carmelita back. I want to go back, not to a new place. Why?"

Anton, one of the four clergy, offered to drive the family of three to the airport in Medellin. Once they approached the airport, Hank could not believe his eyes. He had never seen anything quite like these huge airplanes setting down and lifting off the runways. *"What in the world is this place and what are those huge wing machines? Why are we going in this huge building and why are those men taking my bag with my clothes? This is really weird."*

Inside the terminal, Hank lost his orientation to the aircraft and when they were called to board, he did not realize he had become a passenger inside one of the large jets. *"What a huge room and I have never seen so many people in one place. Who are all these people? Seth is pushing me in this wheelchair he took from someone else – where is my wheelchair? Whoa…what is this little hallway? Everyone is standing around at that little door ahead. Sure was nice they let us move first, but where are we going? Hmmmm..... Seth is picking me up and carrying me inside this little door and look at all these chairs squished together. This is a little bit like a church that we have attended, but this is no church that is for sure."*

Seth deposited Hank in a seat by a little window in the front row then sat down next to him in the middle chair in the row. Lorraine had been right behind carrying a small bag of supplies Hank usually notices when they go to town. As the jet taxied down the runway, Hank began to put things together and realized he was inside the wing vehicle and about to launch. Looking out the small, round window, Hank saw the movement of other winged machines and could not believe his eyes when he saw those other huge machines line up on the street and zoom down the runway. Before he could believe his eyes, they jumped into the air and quickly turned into small birds flying away. Suddenly, a voice bellowed through their winged machine and declared a "take off", whatever that was. Just as quick as he heard the voice, he could feel their machine lurch backward and begin to move until the machine jerked and began moving forward. Hank saw other wing machines change position as he looked out the window. All of a sudden, he realized they were the machine changing position. Buildings and the surroundings were flashing past his window as this huge machine rumbled down the road they were on.

His heart beat a mile a minute – how else do you interpret your first flight after seeing a jet for the first time less than an hour ago. Suddenly a force came over the machine and Hank thought "I have been in cars and Papi's truck when they moved, this is different, and I have never ridden with so many people at once. This wing thing is going faster than cars and the side of the road is getting blurry" …..then……lift off.

"Holy Father God, what is going on?" This was the craziest thing Hank had ever experienced. It was more difficult for Hank to sit in the window seat instead of the aisle, but Seth wanted Hank to get as much from the flight as possible and that meant window. As the passenger jet climbed higher and higher into the sky, Hank was mesmerized by the shrinking features of land and roads below him.

Hank thought to himself, "How am I in the air? What is the reason people do this? Is this for fun, or is there a purpose?" Without more life experience than he had, Hank was unable to project what awaited him. He didn't know enough to question what the backside of this trip would reveal.

What seemed like an eternity in the jet was only 3 hours of air time, but Hank was getting bug eyed as the earth began to get bigger and bigger. Roads and highways returned to focus from the small lines and ribbons he had seen from high above the earth. Buildings became buildings again in place of small blocks and the interesting quilt of patterns defining properties and farms returned to trees, lakes, and fields. "How did all those little things become huge so quickly?" Hank did not know how to process that he had been on a 1000-mile journey in the air and had been transported to New

Orleans in the United States. In his mind, *"what part of Columbia is this?"* could not be expressed, let alone could Hank realize he was not in Columbia anymore.

Seth and Lorraine transferred Hank from his seat to an airline wheelchair and pushed him into the Louis Armstrong terminal. Pushing him to the next terminal for the second flight to Birmingham was no different than the time spent in the airport in Medellin. People dressed a little differently and some of the images and signage were different, but Hank had such a limited reading vocabulary that the difference in languages did not register.

Lorraine walked to a counter and bought everyone something to eat and drink. She returned with some unrecognizable food. Hank was really hungry while Lorraine cut his hamburger into small pieces and broke his French fries in half to feed him. She smiled at Hank as she helped him and he thought back to his mami' LaNita. As much as he appreciated Lorraine and Seth, he missed his family more than anyone understood. This trip was not a positive experience - but with the limitation in Hank's expression, no one really thought to explore what he was going through. Sitting in this new airport was beyond Hank's comprehension. He was so lost geographically he did not realize how far removed from his "home" reality that this spot in New Orleans amounted to.

About an hour and a half passed and Seth wheeled Hank around in the temporary chair. The three of them made way to another part of the terminal. Seth approached the agent at a tall counter and returned with a special pass for the family. In about 20 minutes, Seth got behind Hank and pushed him into another tunnel and transferred him to a new seat in another jet. Hank got it this time. *"But where was this thing taking me? Another trip, but what is the purpose of this. What is happening this time?"* Before long, the Grissom's had returned to their home state of Alabama and landed in the Shuttlesworth Airport in Birmingham. Hank's mind just spun like a hamster wheel - *"what part of Columbia is this?"*

The journey was not complete. Seth greeted a strange man and woman from the Arisen Son Church in Tuscaloosa, and everyone exchanged hugs and back pats. Then the young man greeting Seth and Lorraine turned to me and mentioned my name along with some additional conversation. Chuck put out his hand to shake my hand which I clumsily attempted to get out from under a blanket Lorraine had draped over me. When Seth had transferred me to the temporary wheelchair (which was way too big for me) I had been deposited on my right hip and was falling onto my right arm. In addition to being tangled in the blanket, I was basically pinning my arm to the chair side. Chuck was visibly uncomfortable interacting with me and withdrew his hand and lunged in for a hug in its place. As short as the hug was, Chuck pulled away and I slipped further into the side of the chair.

Marie, Chuck's wife, noticed Hank's poor posture and came to his rescue. After reaching under Hank's arms and pulling him up into a legitimate sitting position, she stepped back and quickly knelt in front of Hank's chair. Marie made sure to make eye contact with Hank which was easier when she crouched down. Marie reached over to touch Hank's arm and gently caressed his arm. "I bet you are worn out from the travel and don't have any idea of where you are? Welcome to Alabama!" Hank was relieved to have someone at least acknowledge his circumstances. "I hope Marie is a good friend of the family" Hank thought to himself as he breathed a sigh of relief. He was beginning to piece together that this day of travel may be reaching an end.

Chuck and Seth retrieved the luggage from the baggage claim while Lorraine and Marie made small talk. Marie went out of her way to welcome Hank and frequently turned to him with a comment. Hank felt out of place and could not respond to Marie, but she braved through the awkward nature of his silence and routinely leaned in to rub his shoulders or grab his hand. Hank felt uncomfortable the first few comments, but soon realized no response was needed. Marie only wanted to provide Hank comfort. She could feel him relax more with each physical gesture and Hank couldn't remember this amount of reassurance since his days of playing and being looked after by sister Carmelita. Hank knew this was a permanent change and didn't comprehend much of anything happening to or around him. Hank felt the connection with Marie in about 30 minutes and began to accept the changes he knew were in store.

Before long, Seth had gotten Hank's personal chair and exchanged chairs for him. Chuck had stepped out to retrieve his Ford Explorer to load luggage and passengers for the final leg of this trip. Hank could not wait to get somewhere and become situated in a new home. As they began passing through Birmingham, Hank could not help but compare the buildings and roads to what he was familiar with in Medellin. As the Explorer rolled out of the city, Hank made note of the similarities and differences in buildings and houses that popped up in the distance from the road. One thing that did come to mind was how far away the homes seemed to cluster from the highway. Growing up in El Ocaso, Hank was not used to 6-lane highways running through the countryside.

35

Money Wire

Before the Grissoms departed La Quiebra, Seth had arranged for the transfer of Hank's wealth from Columbia to the Best Bank in Tuscaloosa. This was the personal bank for Seth and Lorraine as well as the bank for their church. When the insurance company had settled the benefit payout for Hank, Seth had arranged for the funds to be deposited in an account for Hank. Transferring this large amount of money into the U.S. required some doing on the part of the insurance company. At the time of the transfer, U.S. tax codes exempted the deposit from taxes since this particular amount of wealth was derived from an insurance payout. This clearly wasn't on Carlos' mind when the policies were established, but this share of the funding entered Best Bank in the simplest manner imaginable.

Hank's benefits had been sitting in the account churning up a meager return on investment until the family was physically present to make some decisions on a more lucrative profile in the stock market. The three insurance policies totaled $300,000 which was sitting in the Bank the last years prior to Grissom's return to the country. Even with the ridiculously small interest return, by the time Seth arrived and checked on the account, the balance had grown to just over $337,000. As a precaution, Seth had reached out to an attorney in Tuscaloosa, Leon Travers, to serve as custodian of the account.

Leon also had responsibility for reporting interest and growth to the IRS. Seth could check on the account and represent Hank in investment decisions, but no withdrawals could be made without Mr. Travers co-signature.

Travers met with Seth and Hank to review options to best invest Hank's growing fortune. Decisions were made to place the bulk of the account in a brokerage firm in a series of ETFs to diversify the funds. Best Bank continued to hold $100,000 in staggered certificates of deposit which would free the base amount plus growth every 6 months allowing spending cash if Hank made a purchase decision. $30,000 of the $100,000 remained in a money market account which could be withdrawn at any time regardless of the calendar on a CD. Hank seemed to be overwhelmed with the understanding of his wealth and opportunity. Before tying up all his investments, a collective decision was made to purchase a converted Ford Explorer which included an automatic ramp allowing an electronic wheelchair to roll into place for transport.

Seth and Leon worked to transfer the stash Carlos had placed under the flooring which had been deposited for Hank in a Columbian bank. When the wired funding from the Columbia account hit the Best Bank account, it added 25% more to Hank's value. Cash value of the transfer was $98,000 after some sound investment within the bank in Columbia. The bank had allowed for a dual holding in the bank and Mutual funds reflecting economic advances in the Columbian economy which had gone through some very impressive developments in the final years of the Grissom's mission appointment. Mr. Travers duplicated the placement of money in AmeriTrade ETF accounts to maximize the value of Hank's holdings. In addition, Leon had begun to pave the transfer of this cash account four months before the actual transfer. Travers experienced some major issues with the cash coming into Hank's possession, the amount of tax that would be levied on a minor who had gained citizenship via adoption in another country, and negotiation of international monetary policies. The complications were significant, but Leon was up to the task and had bought into the overall mission of supporting Hank after all he had endured.

Travers fashioned a Trust account for Hank which designated him the primary owner of all funding. In the event of his death, one third of the funds were transferred to Seth and Lorraine, another third went to the Arisen Son Church in La Quiebra, and the final third would be assigned to a local organization to be determined. This unknown organization would be an entity which provided assistance to Hank and improved his quality of life. With his limited awareness of finances, Hank had a clause in the Trust that established an advisory board composed of Seth or Lorraine Grissom, and two community members to be determined that would have no vested interest in the funds.

36

Time (Doesn't) Flies

Life with Seth and Lorraine was awesome. The nice house and neighborhood they lived in was nothing like Hank had experienced in El Ocaso. Nothing could replace his family, but Seth and Lorraine were about as close to a replacement as anyone could have dreamed up. Hank was fed every day as if it were a banquet compared to what he was accustomed to.

Then there was the wardrobe for Hank. After Lorraine had outfitted him for the funeral service, Hank began to pick out the white shirt and tie as his go to outfit. Seth and Lorraine took care of him and got him dressed in really styled up clothes. His closet was filled with the majority of shirts white, pale blue, occasional pink, and solid grey. Each shirt color was matched with at least four coordinated ties or bowties. As a measure of efficiency, the ties and bowties were clip-ons and bowties began to take precedent since they stayed out of Hank's way and he just liked the look. Hank appreciated that he fit in with other youth even if he didn't fit in. Middle school is an awkward age if there ever was an awkward age. The formal outfits Hank wore to school were a statement to everyone that he meant business and projected ability and capacity. The students in his school would often comment to Hank about his wardrobe, but Hank couldn't reply.

Seth was great about taking Hank to athletic events at his school and at the University in town, but it was always a passive event. Hank could really get into the competition on the court or on the field, but no one ever knew. Nothing was intentional, but shortly after getting to an event, Seth would be recognized by someone from church and fall into a conversation with them at Hank's expense. Seth kept his hand on the handle of Hank's wheelchair and constantly rolled him in a small arc of movement on the wheels, but it was more a habit than attention.

Lorraine would always look for movies she thought he would like and take him to the theater or occasionally to a concert at the amphitheater. Hank made his best effort to get into songs by rocking himself in the wheelchair, but Lorraine was usually more engaged in the songs than Hank. By the time she asked if he was having fun, he had completed his imaginary dancing and she would reply, "I bet you loved that!"

Hank was preoccupied with programming on tv when at home. Either Seth or Lorraine would channel surf for a while and out of courtesy ask, "Is this something you would like?" before changing the channel. For some reason not clear to Hank, they would usually stop on a cartoon or underage programming that was better than nothing, but not a choice Hank would make. Just another part of the stereotype Hank had to live out when people would make decisions for him based on a perception of inability and limited to no intelligence. "Sigh," Hank thought, "why couldn't they leave the channel with the cars on? Why can't they realize I really like the Sci-Fi station and the mystery programming that taps my imagination?" He was thankful for this couple and this new land and home to live in. Hank appreciated things more than anyone seemed to know.

37

Mounting Evidence

Cy Reeder had plenty of distractions to take him off the abandoned Yamaha Li case, but his hunch that this could lead to a drug bust maintained his interest. Data base entries always had a date of entry for the event of interest. Finding an abandoned water cycle in Destin coincided with the date of a reported missing person. Family of Martino Randalso had reported him missing within 24 hours of the abandoned Yamaha sea vehicle being found.

Cy decided to reach out to the family and determine if they had been able to get any closure. Given the political climate at the time and the presumption of guilt when deporting Latino families, the Randalsos were cautious about talking to a federal authority. They did listen and once they were convinced Cy was sincere about finding information on Martino, a discussion ensued. Gradually they revealed what a family man Martino was and how proud he was of his work in construction. He took great pleasure in consistently getting to his job on time and was a devoted family man. Everything the family shared with Cy pointed to foul play since he was portrayed as dependable, consistent, reliable, and committed to family. They were as bewildered as anyone that Martino had gone missing and had not turned up.

Cy had maintained communications with Sebastian in the

Medellin Police Force and Sebastian helped piece together components of the foreign sea vehicle that had turned up in Destin, Florida. Sebastian's crime board pretty clearly associated the timing of the last citing of Faustino Carbona, the brutal murder of the Carlos Gantera family, and the appearance of the Yamaha sea horse. Pretty amazing that the simplest and inanimate of the three was serving as the common denominator and driving force. Sebastian had set up his board with pictures, reports, names, locations, dates posted on a large bulletin area in his office at the station. Everything was pinned and tied together with string to make a web of activity that would eventually funnel attention to fewer and fewer variables. You have probably seen the configuration on any one of the thousands of detective shows on tv.

Cy had maintained his set of circumstances on a similar board in his office. Some cases will just not go away, and this was one of those. Sebastian and Cy had just recently decided to snap a picture of each other's board and exchange efforts in emails. Each board had a greater emphasis on local details than the other, but common elements surfaced automatically. This comparison was intended to perk features that seemed more subtle to Cy or Sebastian respectively. Exchanges were made approximately 6 months at a time and the ensuing phone calls were rich opportunities to strengthen or weaken evidence revealing the most promising patterns. Over and over discussions between the two investigators pointed strongly at the presence of Faustino Carbona departing Columbia and entering the United States.

Cy was convinced that Carbona was also tied to the disappearance of Martino Randolsa. A body was not produced to confirm Randolsa and Carbona were linked, but Reeder's board made the probability almost a certainty. Cy and Sebastian decided it was time to step up the search and Cy declared Carbona as a Most Wanted fugitive, suspected murderer, and drug dealer. A reward of $2 million dollars was posted with the notice and caution was noted that Faustino Carbona was armed and dangerous. This stepped up the game to involve the FBI network nationwide.

Cy Reeder just had an intuition that the case was close to being solved and he wanted to bring this criminal to justice. Declaring Most Wanted status was essential to open the eyes of more localities that hopefully would result in someone matching the face on the poster to someone in a community. Unknown to Cy was the extreme difference in *The Snowman*'s current look and the picture and sketch integrated into the posters. Posting the notice for Faustino Carbona a.k.a Martino Randolsa proved to be critical in the further narrowing of the search.

Almost two years had passed since the investigation had begun. Associating the names and making entry into the FBI search database scaled the investigation down to five locations where Martino Randolsa had transacted business in the past three years. Alabama, California, Florida, New Mexico, and Texas immediately hit the radar. Cy had decided to make the leap and treat Randolsa and Carbona as one individual. Faustino Carbona did not materialize anywhere. Martino Randolsa was going to get a good review with no stone unturned.

Alabama was payment posted on a Randolsa credit card for lodging in a hotel in Columbia over a three-week period of time. California turned out to be an internet transaction for a bed cover for a pick-up truck with shipping made to Fort Walton Beach, Florida. Florida was the most heavily marked state with a multitude of purchases tagged to two mailing addresses in and around Destin. One residence was posted in Crestview and was the oldest compared to a current residence in Fort Walton Beach. All kinds of transactions were posted against the Fort Walton address and those were all dated over the previous year and a half. About a third as many purchases associated with Randolsa traced back to the Crestview address with the majority of purchases made at a supermarket and many for gasoline at an area Tom Thumb station. New Mexico transactions matched up closely with Texas which were few and appeared to be related to a driving trip based upon date and time of purchases. An equal number and amount of fuel was purchased one week apart indicating travel into Texas and New Mexico and a return trip.

Cy also took note of another citing on the database for a 2010 Ford Ranger that had been abandoned in Destin, Florida and returned to the Randolsa family in Fort Walton Beach. Cy pushed his pins on the investigation board for California, New Mexico, and Texas off to the side. The bulk of the pins in the panhandle of Florida and lower Alabama jumped off the board. Time to make a trip and see things firsthand.

Cy booked a flight into Tallahassee, Florida and arranged for an agent from that outpost to pick him up. Cy had access to a vehicle from the FBI fleet out of Tallahassee for the duration of his investigation. Two years was a significant amount of time to pass for anyone to pick up a trail, but this was not a search for dead bodies and missing weapons. Cy needed to find a live body with a bad history under another name. He didn't waste any time as he headed southwest to Destin. Cy pulled into town around 2:30 pm and sought out the construction company that had employed Martino.

The construction supervisor on the high-rise condominium was available strictly by chance. Completion of the condo was scheduled within two weeks and the super was on site only to confirm completion of some key remedies on a lengthy punch list. He needed to see the finish work first hand to sign off and was only on hand once a week and that was on a Wednesday. Cy asked a series of questions to determine a character portrait for Martino. The super only had a half hour to spare and Cy finished up in 15 minutes. This phase was pretty much a process of elimination to affirm the absence of Martino. Describing Martino was pretty easy – most dependable, very versatile, hard worker, self-starter requiring minimal oversight and due for a promotion until he vanished into thin air.

Next stop was a call on the Randolsa family in Fort Walton Beach 25 minutes away. He thought through the issues he needed to discuss with the family on the drive. He pulled up to the modest home on the north side of town and knocked on the door. Cy would have called ahead if he hadn't recalled how anxious the wife had been over the phone. This was nothing to do with any question of migrant status and he wanted to minimize the chance of making them think that was an issue and to go into hiding despite their legal status. The Ford Ranger with a bed cover was parked in front of the home – check. After making small talk, Cy asked about any knowledge of travel into Texas and New Mexico. As it turned out the family had made the trip and the general dates the Mrs. could recall matched the apparent vacation Cy had assembled in his head – check and check. When asked if they had heard anything at all from Martino, his wife began to cry and blubbered out her disbelief that he would ever abandon the family. Nothing about his disappearance made sense. "One final question, were you aware of any time Martino would have spent in south Alabama?"

"When?" asked the wife.

"Within 24 hours of his disappearance for approximately three weeks" replied the agent.

Mrs. Randolsa had managed to compose herself, she explained that they had located in Fort Walton Beach from Crestview after immigrating and gaining citizenship (emphasis on legal) and they were really unfamiliar with anyone outside the local community.

Cy deduced that Martino was not a negligent parent, not an unfaithful spouse, and his attention needed to focus on where "Martino Randolsa" was currently located. Next stop, last dated transaction, Motel 6, Columbia, Alabama. Cy had visions of staying in small town Alabama and did not particularly care for what he thought he would find. Since the hour was past 6, he decided to unwind with a drink or two, a full meal, and find a decent hotel to stay in. No question in his mind that this resort area of the Florida panhandle was going to be a better experience than his next destination. He settled into his room after dinner and made the most of his night of sleep.

First thing in the morning Cy grabbed breakfast from the complimentary buffet at the hotel and turned the SUV toward Alabama. There was no way for him to know he followed the meandering path of Faustino, but he was pretty close to the same journey. Travel from the south into Columbia did not leave a lot of options. He pulled into Motel 6 in Columbia at 9:45 a.m. and introduced himself to the desk clerk which included flashing the badge. The clerk immediately got serious and was overly accommodating. Lodging records from Faustino's Martino stay were fished from the online registration.

Lynette had been the day clerk at Motel 6 for over 10 years and she said it would be hard to recall people that far into the past. She did, however, see the three week stay which stood out from other guests. "Yes, as a matter of fact, I do remember a long stay by this guy. Pretty much stayed to himself from check in to check out. I'd see him walking across the parking lot a couple times a day heading out on the town. He stayed to himself and seemed to avoid standing out. Only conversations I had with him were check in and check out. I had the card impression at check in and he said it would be an extended stay. I wasn't worried about capturing the fees. I stand in for Mary, our housekeeper, if she doesn't show. I recall making up his room one time and did not see anything out of the ordinary. Guy seemed like a light traveler."

"Can you describe him for me? That is if you can think back that far." Asked Cy.

"Oh, for sure. Dude was a real different looking character. Shaved head and no eyebrows. Patch over his left eye. Pretty ragged looking beard that was full grown and it had to have been dyed, no natural hair looks like mustard. Dressed casual in shorts or jeans and always had a long sleeve shirt or long sleeve sun barrier pullover. Most people around here don't worry about the sun and go short sleeve or no sleeve. Yep, that was his look. And he had the thickest accent I have ever heard. Think he was Mexican, but I had trouble understanding some of what he said. Again, didn't talk much." Lynette would have been a dream witness for a sketch specialist.

Cy was thinking hard about the description. His mind drifted to the profile posted on the "Most Wanted" and these were two different people. At least they looked like two different people. "Anyone else you can suggest that may know more? Were you aware of any people he visited with or met with frequently?"

Lynette thought for a minute and came up with three people to chat with for another perspective. "The two police officers for the town and the waitress staff at Tamala's across the street. Police were on that guy like white on rice and he ate almost every meal at *Tamala's*. Faye and Josette are the waitresses at the restaurant, and they will talk your ear off. Imagine you could get a lot out of them."

Cy thanked Lynette, left a card behind in the event she thought of anything else, and spun around to exit the door. Parked outside Motel 6 next to the black SUV with federal government license plates was officer Willie Whitestone who was chomping at the bit to talk to a "govmant" agent. Willie corroborated Lynette's description of Martino and told Cy "he didn't need to worry – they was keepin uh eye on that migunt. Didn't like the looks of him and tailed him all over town," as if tracking around Columbia, Alabama was a chore. Other than matching descriptions with Lynette, the only benefit Willie supplied Cy was to narrow the waitress interrogation to Josette. "Yeah, the low grade mussa had a thing for Josette. In there shootin the breeze wiff her ever day, sumtime twice a day. An I heered he was a big spender tippin Josette a bunch" explained Willie as if he was cracking a case single handed.

Cy repeated the business card exchange.

"Doan you werry Agent Reeder, he shows up in town aggin, I'll take 'im down an lock his sorry azz up! You can coun' on me. He'z a marked man......low life....." muttered Willie.

Cy walked across the street thinking to himself, "not gonna worry about you helping out Willie, not gonna worry."

Cy cracked the door to **Tamala's** and grabbed a seat.

The waitress strolled over and Faye winked and asked "What can I do ya for?"

Cy saw the nametag, slid his business card on to the table, and explained that he needed to talk with Josette if she was free. Once Faye digested the FBI on the card she back tracked and said Josette would be right out to take his order.

"Yes sir, what can I do for you sir? I didn't do nothin' sir" stammered Josette.

"Please relax Josette, if you can, sit for a few minutes, but first, can I place an order, I am starving. What do you recommend?" Cy inquired.

"Yes sir. Our best seller is the stacked brisket platter. Smoke the meat all day with hickory chips. Comes with steak fries and butter beans, sir. Glad to sub the sides for you, sir. Can't go wrong with the nanner puddin' either, sir."

Cy noticed sweat beading down her forehead, so he tried to put her at ease. "Josette, you have done nothing wrong, so please relax. I have some questions about a customer that frequented your restaurant daily for a few weeks. The hard part is that this man ate here two years ago and may not have been back since then. Martino Randolsa is the customer, maybe you can jog your memory while you bring me that brisket platter and a glass of water."

"Yes sir. I'll get that right up sir. I'll be right back sir" Josette could not lower her anxiety after Faye told her that "an FBI guy was on to her for somethin' an' he's askin' to terragate you". Josette spun around and more or less marched to the kitchen to place the order. While in the kitchen, she poured herself a cold lemonade and chugged the drink down in a long gulp. The cold liquid helped calm her a little, but she wished the drink was some of her husband's booze stash for the weekends. That would have steadied her immediately. "Come on Josette, this is not about you" she thought to herself.

While the plate was being prepared, Josette returned to Cy's table with a place setting and large glass of ice water. Cy asked her to sit if she could. It had just turned 11 a m and he was the only customer in the restaurant, so she could. Lunch crowd shouldn't arrive until close to noon. They began to chat and once the discussion shifted to Martino, Josette recalled the excessive tips he paid and warmed up to Cy while cooling off the anxiety. First order of business for Cy was to once again confirm the description of "Martino". Josette nailed the facial description. She was pretty confident of the height she provided since she could recall his stature standing next to the counter and register. He was about 6 inches taller than the register and on the thin side. On the way out, Cy borrowed a measuring tape and decided he was 5' 8" from her description. Together they arrived at 150-160 pounds. She did add one critical detail to the descriptions. Josette said that this customer would pull up his long sleeves when they would sit and chat and particularly while he ate. She described a goofy looking tatoo of a snowman on his inner left forearm. BINGO!! Columbian authorities had made mention of *The Snowman* and this trademark self-styled tattoo. Cy immediately moved from hunch to manhunt.

Cy started probing for any details he may have shared about a destination since it was pretty clear the suspect had left the area. Josette offered her best guess that "he most likely moved to Tuscaloosa or some place near there. Martino was curious about the Auburn University or University of Alabama fans in town and how it separated people. When I described the two towns for him, he kept asking questions about Tuscaloosa and always referred to Auburn as the small town. He acted like he needed a bigger place to live for some reason. If I wanted to get in touch with him, my money would be on Tuscaloosa."

Armed with these new details and a new facial image to look for, Cy began to gear up for a trip to Tuscaloosa. He had some book work to log into the FBI database and he had the impression the trip north on the backroads of Alabama would use up a good portion of the day. He kicked back at his Motel 6 room he had rented, mostly to coax info out of Lynette. He could have written off the lodging and found a more upscale hotel in another town, but he had a lot to think over and wanted to have his hands free to write or keyboard if things came together. Driving required both hands and attentive eyeballs.

38

Special Customers

Integrating a new country was a bit more complicated than *The Snowman* first thought. Tino spent almost a month tacking across the Florida panhandle and realizing he underestimated his conspicuous presence in small towns. Faustino knew he needed to assimilate into the Tuscaloosa community. He really hoped his presence would not be as conspicuous to the local citizens of a larger and more diverse town than Columbia. Faustino spent six months in Tuscaloosa structuring the US drug network. It would serve him well to have a job and make use of the identity that he had stolen from Martino. *The Snowman* looked through the local want ads for open positions. Salary was really not a concern for him since he had a steady flow of income from the back channels in his drug empire. Whenever necessary he knew to send a text and someone in the drug smuggling network would make a drop of cash. Employment, coupled with Martino's papers, would cover his illegal immigrant status. Since Trump had been in office it was very apparent that he would need to demonstrate citizenship.

Faustino thought about the construction business that Martino was in, but quite frankly, he didn't want to exert himself. He opted instead for some type of work in a dry, air-conditioned environment. His pursuit started with positions in restaurants and food service. His mind drifted back to ***Tamala's*** restaurant and his interactions with Josette. Interacting with locales in that capacity should help him better infiltrate the town. His first job was serving as a busboy at Dillie's Deli. After three months of bussing tables and no indication of advancement, he began to look around town. Tino was pushing a year in the U.S. and needed to spend his work commitment more efficiently in order to rejuvenate his drug commerce.

Smokeez Bar-B-Que had a notice up for a general position that could handle chopping the smoked meats and working the grill. "Opportunity for Advancement" was the part of the ad that really got his attention. Tino got the job, served his notice at Dillie's and got to work at the smoky restaurant. It may have been an indoor position but working the grill and processing the orders in the back room was hot and isolated. He was not making decisions that panned out to his liking and allowed some flexibility to meet his drug ring subordinates. Tino wanted advancement and let the owner know he was committed to being reliable and hoped his work ethic had registered. He made sure to be on time to work and pushed the orders and processed the food quickly. Even though his accent was a heavy South American dialect, he had made the grade for cash register in three months and was satisfied. The Latino population in town was not huge, but it was substantial and Tino actually became a drawing card for this new clientele to dine at the smokehouse.

Archie, one of the owners, saw the positive impact that Faustino was making and followed up on the request for advancement. Meeting and greeting, collecting orders, and taking payment was a great way to identify regulars and establish his membership in Tuscaloosa. Occasionally *The Snowman* was pushed into duty in the kitchen, but that was a rarity and he overlooked the distaste to build a recommendation for another employer if he needed a change of scenery.

Tino was selective with the customers he wanted to befriend since he didn't need anyone to begin snooping into his background. He avoided women because he did not want to answer to their probing efforts to clear his reputation. That was not what he was looking for, he only wanted better opportunities to cover his time and continue the distribution of his drug smuggling free of detection. If companionship was needed, Tino would make the quick trip to Birmingham and frequent a few bars where the ladies were open to his partnership. He made sure not to maintain any long-term relations and avoid the tendency to pry into his background. Tino had a straightforward line to use if his background came into question. If he bumped into a lady friend the third time, he was heading to another bar.

The Snowman cobbled together about a year and a half of time Smokeez which he felt was necessary before exploring any new job opportunities. He was very dependable, and his employment was guaranteed as long as he was interested. Not that he was looking around, but an opportunity presented itself in the most unpredictable manner. Working the lunch shift was usually a rushed couple of hours but prep leading up to noon and clean up afterward made up for the hectic pace when customers would overload the restaurant. Fridays tended to be a busier time than the rest of the week, but during the springtime, even Friday was a slower day…..except for this Friday. Time had clicked off the clock closing in on 1 pm when a busload from the CentrePoint Life, a supported living center pulled into the parking lot. Most of the people exited the bus independently and rushed into the restaurant. A couple of the passengers needed extra support from the bus driver as well as one of the staff from CentrePoint Life to navigate the steps off the vehicle. As the first wave of people pressed through the door of the restaurant and made passage to the counter for their orders, Faustino was struck by features of people he had not experienced. Something looked different about this crowd and Tino couldn't put his finger on what it was. They just looked a little different and quite frankly, none of them really spoke in a manner that he could understand.

This Friday, CentrePoint Life had chosen **Smokeez BBQ** for a lunch on the town since it was conveniently located near the movie theater. Over a dozen people had crowded up to the counter and everyone seemed to be talking simultaneously. Tino couldn't make out anything that was shouted since everyone was interested in a different dish. He was about to hit panic mode from the overload of orders when the staff member appeared from the mass of humanity. The staff member quickly quieted everyone and cautioned them to wait their turn. The chaos died down and Bev, the staff person, introduced herself to Tino and apologized for the confusion and disorganization. She had a quick explanation down pat to orient people to CentrePoint Life and the clientele to transition the group into new surroundings. Most of this went over Tino's head, but he did pick up on the barriers to placing orders and limited communication from a number of these customers. In fact, as the orders began to be processed, and he realized almost everyone needed assistance from Bev, Tino became intrigued.

All the orders were quickly filled since the menu on the wall was really pretty limited. Once Bev stepped up to provide interpretation, Tino could get back to normal. As orders were placed, each person would grab a number tent to sit on the table and orient the server, which today was none other than Tino. *The Snowman* delivered the plastic food baskets lined with wax paper to the respective order number. Every customer was very thankful for their order and muttered thank you or in the case of about half, gave a smile and a thumb up gesture. As the food consumption ramped up, the noise volume abated. Tino stopped at the table that Bev shared with three customers from the bus. He struck up a conversation with Bev and asked to know more about CentrePoint Life. He found out that these people lived in CentrePoint Life and were placed there because families really could not keep up with their needs and a few had actually lost their parents and needed a roof and someone to provide care. Tino was awestruck with the group of people wolfing down their food as the bus driver and Bev occasionally cautioned one of the group to slow down so they did not choke. Time did not allow her to delve into all his questions, so Bev shared a business card with him and invited him to visit CentrePoint Life if he was interested in knowing more. Tino carefully tucked the card into his wallet and allowed his mind to free fall into this group of people who appeared not to be able to communicate independently.

Tino worked through the weekend but typically had Tuesday and Wednesday off to make up for his time. In essence, his weekend was midweek which served a lot of his business needs. Different members of the drug ring would make their way to Tuscaloosa to discuss the REAL business on different weeks. *The Snowman* made sure to stagger his henchmen over the course of a month or so to avoid anyone building any association within the drug line. In addition to talking with *The Snowman* about business, it was pretty generally understood that they would swing by the restaurant and get some of the smoked meat. Everyone wanted some Smokeez and the network employees were no different. Inevitably, the discussion at the restaurant between Tino and his employees would shift to the drug business and *The Snowman* was always anxious and would begin to whisper or talk softly in order not to be heard. Unknown to Tino or his associates, their low murmurs were more conspicuous than if they were talking louder than normal. *The Snowman* had been tiptoeing around drug distribution for over a year and a half and it was beginning to take its toll on his attitude. Tino knew he needed to curtail drug discussions at work and had been thinking things through for weeks before Bev and the bus pulled up that Friday.

39

Putting on a Show

Tuesday rolled around, *The Snowman* was off for the day and he could not wait to make his way to the CentrePoint facility to get a better understanding of the operation. He parked the car, entered the front door and was locked out as he stood face to face with a receptionist behind a plexiglass window seated about 8 feet away. Much like a movie theater ticket window, the plexiglass had a semicircle cut into the bottom of the window. Tino found himself bending over to talk to the receptionist as he asked to visit with Bev. Finally, the receptionist told Tino to push the button on the wall. This did not immediately make sense to Tino, why would a wall have a button? Once his confusion registered with the receptionist, she told him to follow the arrow. A sign was attached to the wall above a buzzer button and he activated the switch which she had released and the door popped open enough to slide his fingers in and open the door. She asked for an ID which Tino flashed in front of her to display the driver's license from his dead persona, Martino. As he had been directed, he turned right down the hallway to the second office. Bev had been paged by the receptionist and rose to greet Tino as he knocked on the doorframe. She was surprised to see the man from the restaurant had followed through on her invitation.

Bev led *The Snowman* on a walking tour of CentrePoint Life

and grounds. Everywhere he looked residents were in their rooms or in common areas watching television or receiving some type of crafts instruction for hobbies. Occasionally they would stumble upon someone mindlessly playing a video game, but Tino could not help but notice very little interaction occurring. This was the trait he noticed during the visit to Smokeez. What made an impression on Tino in the restaurant was the fact that very few people seemed to interact and understand one another. Limited communication or no communication was just what *The Snowman* needed for his drug business. As long as he could not discern any dialogue, he was more confident that he could place orders and interact with his subordinates without being identified.

They turned a corner in the facility and walked down a last corridor that seemed eerily quiet. As they peered into various doorways, Bev explained that this particular wing of the facility was devoted to individuals with dementia, Alzheimer's, and a few people transitioning from a hospital to home that were being dosed with medications for a period of time that warranted nursing care. All Tino heard was dementia and Alzheimer's allowing him to jump to the conclusion that he was never going to be concerned about being discovered in this wing. Who would believe one of these patients remarking that a drug lord was serving them. Almost as if on cue, an alarm went off when one of the "runners" decided to bolt from their room. Bev quickly intercepted the purported escapee and steered them back to their quarters and talked them out of their departure. Tino could feel the glee filling his body as his confidence burst into being. No one would have a clue what he was doing on the side if he stayed away from other staff. Jackpot!!

Bev deliberately did not show one of the wings of the building to Tino. A portion of CentrePoint Life was devoted to serving Court Appointed youth with behavior and emotional disorders. Things could get loud in that unit and the noise and bickering back and forth would send the wrong impression. Bev was not proud of the clientele and kept them under wraps unless someone specifically asked for a tour of that program. Typically, educators and faculty from the university were the only people looking for information or exposure to these delinquents.

As the tour drew to a close, Tino began to shift the focus from an interested visitor to a prospective employee. He knew how to play up the altruistic drive to "help" people. Whatever needed to be said to impress Bev that he was a faithful employee would be stated. Bev said she would let him know if any positions would open since the only work currently available was to serve as a patient orderly. Bev had overestimated Tino's drive and suspected he was only interested in a paraprofessional position that would allow him more time with the residents in the Centre. *The Snowman* assured her that he wanted to help in any way and that orderly responsibilities would be a fine starting point. He simply wanted to serve people with limitations that could not help themselves. Bev tried to talk him out of the position, but Tino persisted until she offered him an application to fill out. The patient orderly position was in the behavior and emotional needs wing and Tino was unaware it existed.

40

SPECIAL EDUCATION?

Hank was enrolled in a local middle school and placed in special education with a condition of Intellectual Disability (*code for they do not think I am smart*). The Individual Education Plan (IEP) that was written for Hank included service with a physical therapist and an occupational therapist, which he greatly appreciated. No attention was devoted to his communication barriers. (*who are the professionals here?*) Lorraine, as an adoptive parent, had served as his advocate to secure services for his many needs. No fault of her own, Lorraine did not know to ask for communication development. Speech Pathology would have been the logical service provider, but without speech, people tend to think communication is not realistic. This would have been the biggest piece of the puzzle for Hank, but for the time being, that card was left out of the deck.

Lacking the history of being a parent, neither Lorraine nor Seth thought of building Hank's school communication through a system separate from speaking. They had eventually done such a good job building his card communication system, it seemed only natural that they would make that a condition of his program. Being new to parenthood and starting things up at age 13, neither Seth nor Lorraine knew the IEP process. Both parents assumed that the special educators would volunteer the services needed. Ms. Gesslinger assumed the parents would request language services if he was accustomed to them. And Hank, he was caught right in the middle of the assumptions. Assume makes an "ass out of u and me" in most cases. It sort of applied to both adult sides of this equation, but Hank was back to being treated as a deaf mute……… Sigh !!!

Hank understood how people could gloss over his capacity to develop communication. He was too forgiving, but in the immediate circumstance, what could he do. The longer communication was neglected, the further Hank was from developing a means to let people know his needs and thoughts. As backward as it was, the school kept Hank in a secluded room on the outskirts of the school campus. Hank was taught the little bit that was provided him in a portable trailer classroom. Hank was the afterthought of a student in the afterthought of a classroom by the afterthought of a teacher (Ms. Gesslinger). Gesslinger was an aging physical education teacher that could no longer keep up with the oversized classes of students she was assigned in elementary schools. She couldn't have been a kinder person and was a grandmother to all the children in her class. As it turned out, Hank and Ms. Gesslinger were starting special education at the same time. She was trying to outlast the system to complete her retirement pension requirements and the school system "couldn't find" a certified special educator. Ms. Gesslinger accepted the job without thought since it appeared to be nothing more than babysitting five students in wheelchairs. They even gave her a teacher assistant to sip coffee with in the morning during the beginning of the day when Hank and his four classmates sat mindlessly watching a spin-off of Sesame Street.

This was a pretty sad picture for a small group of primary grade students who could not voice their needs and interests. Unfortunately, Hank and his buds were not primary age and had been given up on long ago. If they were to have any life experience at all, they needed the attention a 5:2 student to teacher ratio should indicate.

In addition, Hank and his posse needed to be seen by the rest of the school and be understood. Hank needed to be among the general population building a network of friends and supports for his future. Life just wasn't fair. The next two years were a lot like being on a treadmill, but at the slowest speed possible. Treadmill travel was endless and worthless at the same time. No outcome and no value - and no speed in this situation.

Lorraine did stay on the lookout for opportunities for Hank and had heard of a local program called PARA (Parks and Recreation Association) that had programming for children and youth with special needs. She did not know much about the organization but figured it would be an opportunity for Hank he needed to try. Lorraine picked an evening event off their schedule and drove Hank to a community center to get a look at the offering. After retrieving the umbrella stroller used for ease of portability, she pulled Hank into place from the car and wheeled him into the building. Once inside, Lorraine was shocked with the number of unique youths in attendance and how lively things were. Everyone from participants through staff were smiling from ear to ear and having the best time you could imagine. They registered at a table near the door and were quickly escorted to a table with a spot open for Hank. Lorraine wheeled the stroller into place then realized there was no seat for her. Talk about walking in Hank's shoes, Lorraine was left out of the fun. After a few seconds that seemed like an eternity, the staff member that registered Hank guided her away from the table and offered two options…..sit in the back with the other parents or go somewhere else to enjoy her free time. She needed to be back to pick up Hank in an hour and a half. Lorraine immediately felt her anxiety kick in as she wondered to herself how Hank could survive without her for over an hour. School was one thing (if she only knew), but this was just too wild. The staffer assured Lorraine all was well and that everyone had a lot of experience providing for the participants. Lorraine gradually assumed the position of peanut gallery with the parents to see what was in store.

Tonight was Karaoke night at PARA and once the system cranked up and the first person started belting out their rendition of "Brick House", the crowd began to cut loose. Dr. Marrell was a member of the organizers and he and Cody were belting out this anthem song for Karaoke. Dr. Marrell made his way among the participants to engage each one while continuing his best bass calling on that Brick House. Cody meanwhile was glued to the system and loved the microphone. Fortunately for the parents Marrell's volume overpowered Cody who sounded a lot like an injured dog howling. This dynamic duo served as the warmup routine for each Karaoke event and they were masters.

Lorraine had never seen anything like this in her life. These poor helpless "children" were coming out of their seats and laughing at almost everything that happened. No one was immune to the happiness and that included Lorraine. Another favorite was Michael Jackson's "Thriller" delivered by Gary. He was followed by Heather crooning her favorite Western tune "Donk, BeDonk, BeDonkey Donk" while entertaining with dance moves never seen before. Heather would have been a natural for the song row in Nashville.

Lorraine noticed one of the "kids" sitting next to Hank encouraging him to accompany him on stage. Lorraine's heart just sunk as she envisioned Hank's embarrassment to be forced into the theatrics. She began to rise out of her chair to rescue Hank when the staff member from the front desk appeared from nowhere and wheeled Hank up to the stage with his new found friend. Hank was handed a mike and his buddy, Bart, had chosen "Dance to the Music" from decades ago to sing along. Hank was able to hold the mike with one hand and push off a table with another as if he was swaying to the song....NAH, Hank was Dancin to the Music and full-fledged rockin out. Occasionally Hank would pull the mike to his mouth and make some unintelligible sound then just flail back and forth in the stroller and put on a special Hank smile. Lorraine was star struck seeing Hank so totally engaged. Seth had to see this next Karaoke Night. This was soooo good!!

At a break in the music, pizza and donuts were brought in for refreshments. Caroline Sears, the staff member that was Hank's go to gal intercepted Lorraine as she began to swoop in to control what Hank would get to eat. Caroline assured Lorraine she had an eye on Hank and Lorraine could relax. One of the parents sitting nearby tugged on Lorraine's arm and diverted her attention. Lorraine was about to begin her education with the parent and sat back down to take things in. Quickly, Lorraine was nodding her head in understanding and compliance as her parent partner explained the need for parents to butt out when PARA was in action. The youth needed their freedom and Caroline was a faculty member from the University and was as capable as anyone in the room at safely letting Hank have some space. Hank was definitely tripping out with the donut holes. Small enough to grab, soft enough to chew, and sugar enough to power him through the next track of tunes.

Everyone returned to their seats as the second session of tunes was about to begin. Some of the songs were so off key and riddled with the wrong words you struggled to identify the song by title. Didn't matter. This was all about the fun and all about engagement. Hank was consumed with the songs, the sounds, the laughter, and the new acquaintances. Best part of all is that no one was phased that Hank could not say things, everyone communicated effortlessly. This was the best night of Hank's life. Come to think of it, best night of Lorraine's life too.

As the event drew to a close, Caroline took the stage and made some announcements about coming events. This weekend PARA was hosting lunch and a movie, which turned out to be "Avengers Endgame". Lorraine was totally bewildered with the choice of movie. Hank had seen tv ads about "Endgame" and he was fidgeting away as excited as he could be. Caroline winked at Hank and made her way over to Lorraine to explain. Lorraine continuously repeated "I don't know....I just don't know" while Caroline gradually talked her down and got a commitment to drop off Hank for lunch Saturday at 11:30. Transportation was arranged to and from CentrePoint Life to the restaurant and theater. The van had a wheelchair lift and Caroline insisted that Hank would be most comfortable in his full-sized chair. As quick as it began, Karaoke was over. Lorraine peered over at Hank strapped into the car with the seat belt and couldn't help but think he was drunk or high on something. In fact, he was, high on life and Karaoke.

41

SiriousXM

Seth and Lorraine were hooked and had the next Karaoke night event marked in their calendars. Hank was beside himself every day waiting for another night of unbridled fun with a bunch of friends incapable of judging. Hank was in his own world of anticipation as he looked forward to the next music event. Seth and Lorraine finally told him another Karaoke was planned and he needed to get his throat warmed up for whatever happened at the PARA program. As they pulled up to the facility, Hank was squirming around in his chair. Seth was just curious since the way Lorraine had described the entertainment left him unable to connect the dots. As soon as Hank got his wheels across the door threshold, he was into entertainment mode. Seth pulled back against the wall to take things in, as did Lorraine while wondering if the peak of excitement Hank displayed was a reality. Within seconds, all questions were answered, and the roof was raising off the foundation. Seth had never experienced anything like this and was fascinated by the amount of engagement that these people with "no ability" performed so valiantly. Seth smiled so hard it was as if his face was going to rip off. What a night, what an education for Seth, and what another step forward for Hank.

Hank was Barry Gibbs this night as the soundtrack for *Saturday Nite Fever* was blaring most of session one. It was ironic for Hank to be mouthing *Fatality* by the BeeGees even though there was no fatality here. Hank was in his realm. Lorraine had unknowingly been training Hank for his song for the past two weeks as she tooled around town with Hank in the car. She was a faithful SiriousXM listener and kept things dialed into channel 7 for the 70's decade of music. The daytime disc jockey was all about the BeeGees with at least one of their songs broadcast each hour. That was just fine with Hank. Lorraine watched him in the rearview mirror displaying his heartwarming grin and rolling his head back and forth to the music.

Lorraine had put in the request for BeeGees tunes and had personally rolled him on stage. They say you can't teach an old dog new tricks, but Lorraine had learned a lifetime of opportunity from Karaoke night one. She was all in on the PARA programming and starting to see so much promise in Hank. Not to be ugly at all, she was all about her inexperience, but Hank had pretty much been a novelty before PARA programming. Hank was Lorraine's mission in life upon returning to the United States. She felt that God had placed Hank in her life to take care of him, to feel sorry for him, and to be his alter ego. Slowly but surely, however, it was becoming obvious that God placed Lorraine and Seth in Hank's life so he could teach them in his ways and open their eyes to his sense of purpose.

42

iPhone to the Rescue

Karaoke was such an abstract event to have made such an impact on the Grissoms. When someone enters into the circle of people with intellectual disabilities, underestimating and not expecting anything is a given. As you read this book, it is difficult to disconnect from the amazing technology supports all individuals have become accustomed to and take for granted. Technology advancements, particularly individual equipment, have become so prevalent that apps have opened eyes to more accurate perception of the Hanks of the world. Let me adjust you to the timeframe in which Hank is situated. Technology and education are just beginning to intersect around 2012. Technology advances to benefit Hank are at the cutting edge - the bleeding edge - as referred by change advocates. Trial and error takes valuable time and resource to marry tech advantage to individual and unique need. The hardest part right now is the means for Hank to interact with the technology. A side benefit of the Karaoke event was the introduction of Caroline Sears to Hank. Caroline had a great intuition about the versatility of an iPhone and what it could mean for Hank. She and Knox Marrell were tech savants and always on the lookout for a way to integrate technology into the lives of their partners with disabilities. Knox was familiar with a student group in electrical engineering on campus and Caroline recruited students in special education at The University of Alabama. These two student groups threw themselves into the challenge and quickly devised a way to position an iPhone on Hank's wheelchair with a selfie stick. An oversized switch was the interface for Hank to click a picture. Even more important, the iPhone was able to translate from Hank's Spanish to English and back again to facilitate interactions. The card-based system was in Spanish since the Grissoms were competent in Spanish, but now that they were in the U.S., English was a huge part of the equation.

Seth had contacted the Alabama Department of Rehabilitation and secured a contemporary motorized wheelchair. The chair allowed Hank to change posture, elevate his seat, and recline the seatback which allowed him to navigate freely without someone making decisions for him. The attachment of the selfie stick was done in such a way that he could angle the camera in the iPhone to select pictures of his interest. Making use of a bracing cushion, Hank was able to stabilize his arm and use his left elbow to bump the controls to modify the position of the iPhone and camera lens. An oversized interface screen had been built into the configuration by the engineering students so Hank could see the screen easier. The enlargement also made more precision adjustments to the screen and focus for Hank. He used a similar bump switch with his right elbow to navigate the chair and travel to his position of interest.

Independent navigation was one factor, but Hank quickly mastered his controls and began to use the phone as a way to build visualization as a communication strategy. Hank was really quite brilliant despite being buried inside his physical disability. Much like many others in his condition, he was classified as intellectually disabled, but he was far from that diagnosis. With the help of Dr. Sears, Dr. Marrell, and the collection of students, he was able to take control of his world in ways not imagined before.

Seth was the first to notice the patterns in his photo portfolio.

Seth used his color card system to interact with Hank and realized the method behind the photo collection. He began to ask Hank to explain....well.....show him how he went about selecting things to photograph and how he would focus and take the pictures. From this humble beginning, Seth gained a tremendous insight into Hank's intellect and realized just how much he had misunderstood. This shift in awareness happened over a period of time mainly because Seth constantly found himself questioning what he was seeing. "How did this photo get Hank's attention? Is this a legitimate selection, or is Hank just lucky?" Eventually, Seth realized he was dealing with a very capable young man with much more to offer than he could imagine. Seth and Lorraine took great interest in sharing this newfound understanding and commissioned Hank to start taking shots for display in the church.

Seth made sure that Hank was with him any time he displayed one of the photos in the church. Credit was given to Hank when anyone interacted with Seth about the portfolio that was developing. Many of the church members showed interest in the photos and very politely acknowledged Hank when Seth began to explain the images. Unfortunately, and unknown to Seth, everyone was giving a nod to the project, but just could not grasp the fact that the photographer was not Seth. Hank was becoming a fixture in the church and members readily approached Hank to share one of his fist bump elbow-to-fist greetings. The general understanding was that Seth was the doting father who could not see his son's limitations. It did not take Seth long to realize that the congregation just could not make the leap and credit Hank with the photos. Seth decided to dig in deeper and find a way to prove Hank's worthiness as a photographer and individual.

43

BANG THE DRUM

An unpredictable pathway emerged from the PARA programming. Seth chatted with Dr. Sears and Dr. Marrell about the dilemma that was emerging at the church. He very much wanted people to come to grips with Hank's unique ability and hidden intellect. Seth forgot how complicated and drawn out his understanding of Hank had taken. Caroline and Knox both encouraged Seth to communicate with Dr. Trianna Mugota on the faculty at The University of Alabama. Dr. Mugota was very knowledgeable of alternate communication strategies which endeared her to Seth and vice versa. Initially, Trianna probed Seth's approach to building the alternative communication system with Hank. She was enamored with the recognition that Seth had come to grips with regarding the use of the iPhone and explained that technology could do much more for Hank than just take photos, although that was an impressive development in her mind. Trianna was aware of a parent conference for families dealing with offspring with intellectual disabilities. An important step in her mind for Seth, Lorraine, and Hank to take would be to affiliate with this group and mine other families for ideas. The one-day families conference was scheduled for the following month in Birmingham and Seth made reservations.

Lorraine continued to learn from the parents in attendance at

PARA. Hank looked forward to each event hosted for peers he had met through Karaoke and the various luncheons. Lorraine noticed that the families conference in Birmingham was scheduled in conflict with the upcoming Karaoke night with PARA. Seth and Lorraine discussed the conflict and decided it would be an important decision for Hank to weigh in. The trio finished up their meal that evening and Seth explained the value of the conference and the conflict with Karaoke.

44

CHRISTMAS SHOPPING, THANK YOU PARA

Hank had just been enrolled in Peabody High School while living with Seth and Lorraine after completing middle school. He had really found a niche in life through the PARA program and looked forward to every bit of program they provided. PARA was the one segment of his life that seemed to allow him to fit into activities and did not jump to conclusions from his silence. He found a new "Bart quality friend" almost every time he attended another activity. Not everyone got what Hank was thinking, but everyone treated him in a respectful way from the first hello to "see you next time". Hank was alive. On one of the shopping trips PARA arranged, he was instructed to find and buy something for his "parents" that would let them know how much he appreciated them. Christmas was approaching and PARA encouraged the participants in the program to be thoughtful for their parents and/or guardians.

Hank's mentor for the day, Grey – a teacher education major – wheeled him into a craft store. Grey had been volunteering 10 hours a week with PARA and he immediately connected with Hank. Grey wheeled Hank around the store and pointed out a number of items that were within the range of pricing compared to Hank's funding. Grey took the liberty to roll Hank into the aisles filled with Christian gifts. Hank perked up when he saw the crosses and seasonal displays of merchandise for purchase. Grey took notice of a shift in Hank's posture and had the distinct impression these gifts were of interest to his shopping partner.

Hank knew how much the church meant to Seth and he found a woven bracelet with a cross where a watch would display if it were a watchband. This was the perfect gift for his new father. This bracelet was a pretty hip looking accessory. Grey liked the find and commented that "I would like this if I was your parent", which registered on Hank. He had seen a lot of people at the church wearing similar bracelets and necklaces from woven cloth or cords. This piece was woven cord that intertwined purple and gold cords then fastened at the cross with a clasp that hooked into a loop at the free end of the cords. The cross was a weathered looking pewter color that appeared to have already been put to the test. The combination of color and texture impressed Hank as a very authentic symbol of the belief he shared with Seth.

Lorraine was an easy gift. The two shoppers looked over a number of prints and paintings on display and found one that reminded Hank of Lorraine. He wasn't sure what kind of bird it was that was flying through a wreath, but it was heading up into parting clouds with the sun piercing through and shining distinct rays of light as if to direct the bird in flight. This imagery seemed so peaceful and – well - heavenly. Hank reflected a bit more on the print and his mind wandered back to his Columbian parents and sister. It did not take much for him to envision them riding with this bird of peace to heaven. Snapping back to the present, he began to point to this particular picture with his elbow which he had better control over than his hand. Grey commented that this too would be an excellent gift for his parent and what a beautiful depiction of heaven it projected. That confirmation was exactly what Hank wanted to hear. He began to rock forwards and backwards in his chair. Grey took the lead and said "Yes, this is what you want to buy?" Hank grunted an affirmative that seemed to register with Grey. "Well, let's go pay for these and we can wait for the others on the trip." Hank shoved the money on a tray on his chair toward Grey who intuitively said "Gotcha" and helped his shopping buddy toward the cashier. Mission accomplished, Hank felt good.

The bus returned to the PARA building and everyone unloaded. The mentors had been told to help their partner as little as possible with gift wrapping. With Hank's limited motor control, that left quite a bit for Grey to do. Grey cut off an appropriate square of paper to wrap around the gift boxes. He used his own hand and arms to block Hank's arms to steady his movements. The paper was clumsily covering the gift boxes as Hank managed a fold using the back of his hand. Grey did a great job of encouraging Hank every fold and tape strip that was applied. When they finished, both wrapped boxes looked as if they had been pinned in the conveyor belt moving packages through the post office. There was really no way to know what was inside the wrapping, but that was a miracle in itself since bare parts of the gift box peered through the paper all around. The tape held, but the multiple strips of tape at each loose end were folded over in the middle of the length where Hank could not control his fine motor movements.

You could imagine a 5-year-old had wrapped these packages from the looks of them, but all it did was add value to the offering. Grey offered Hank a fist bump which Hank met with his forearm. The two had very limited words to say to one another throughout the shopping and wrapping experience, but they had connected. Grey wished Hank a Merry Christmas and told him he hoped to spend more time with him soon. Hank had one of his classic smirky smiles on his face. This was almost as good as Karaoke, almost.

45

SCHOOL NEWSLETTER EDITOR

Life with Seth and Lorraine was good. They had been back in the U.S. for over two years and had really developed a family unit among themselves. Hank thought less and less of Carlos, LaNita, and Carmelita and replaced them with newfound memories of Lorraine and Seth and PARA. His life was so much fuller than ever before, and Hank found new friends at school through some clubs he had been "invited" to attend. These met after school and his teacher, Ms. Gessenger, thought it would be a good experience for her students. She selected clubs based upon her personality matches and submitted their names to the club advisors. Sink or swim would be the Gessenger model for preparation. Not really understanding academic needs for her classroom, she thought the club might be of interest to the students and they may carry projects back to her room to occupy their time. What started out as a ploy to take work off her plate actually turned into a genius move to legitimately include Hank and his peers with the general population of Peabody High.

Hank's club was the school newsletter under the direction of Mr. Murphy, a teacher in the English department. As the advisor, "Murph" knew what an impact the newsletter could have on the school, but he needed the right ingredients to seek out and build quality stories. The newsletter was distributed once a month and featured outstanding efforts from the arts, sports, academics, and always included a Teacher of the Month. Hank quickly sought out ways to demonstrate his photography skills and was befriended by Addie, one of the 11th grade students in the class. Addie was a once in a million student who was respectful and polite among an increasingly radical and rowdy school population. She had become interested in playing soccer at a young age and had become quite skilled and was a major force on the school team. Addie introduced Hank to the soccer team, her class, and always included Hank in parties and saw to it that he would have access to school dances. Time between Hank and Addie served both students well. Hank gained an understanding friend who genuinely enjoyed his company and found ways for him to be involved in school and community events that no one else in his classroom experienced. Their relationship was strictly plutonic, but very special.

With Addie paving the way, Hank had an opportunity to become a celebrity at the school as the dynamic duo would seek out the shining stars and teachers to showcase in the newsletter. Addie would interview, Hank would photograph, and both would edit the work and integrate the pictures into the monthly media. Hank was adept at pointing out some of the less than obvious students who just lurked in the background of school operation. Due to his keen eye, Hank helped discover the talents of Bishop (a budding chef in the culinary club), Landon (a shy cast member in the drama club), Maddy (an abstract painter in the art club), among others. Without fail, Hank could pick a classmate from these clubs that had extraordinary talent but limited exposure. Each of Hank's newsletter subjects were on the fringe of their club membership, but quite capable in their club specialties. Once Addie began to interview these candidates and the two of them built the newsletter profile for select students, these students saw their stature in the school rise. More and more students made pitches to highlight their exceptionality or, more importantly, nominate someone that they thought was flying under the radar and deserved some attention. Without realizing their impact, Addie and Hank transformed the school climate from a bunch of elitists clicks into a very rich, accepting school climate.

Members of the faculty were not immune to the impact of the newsletter. As many student body favorites were featured in the newsletter, the teachers began to take more interest in Hank and his "special ed" class. The end of the year issue was going to include special edition interest stories that were suggested by the faculty. Riding the tails of the newsletter and the publicity, select students and teachers realized unprecedented exposure and popularity. Ironically, the newsletter profiled everyone and everything except the newsletter. Principal Marqueth called a faculty meeting the first week of April to announce a context search for the student with the biggest contribution to Peabody High. Marqueth then called a student assembly and explained his interest in recognizing the faculty or staff member that had done the most for the school that past year. A ballot was created for students to write in their faculty member and class peer that stood head and shoulders above everyone else. Marqueth wanted to assure he would distance himself from the outcome and requested Mr. Woods, one of the elementary school principals to coordinate a tabulation board.

Ballots were printed and distributed April 8th for a one-time election process. One ballot box was located in the main foyer of the school with Mr. Marqueth or one of his Office Support staff monitoring the box. Woods arrived at the end of the school day and picked up the box. When Mr. Woods was asked to help out, Marqueth shared a couple of months of the newsletter with him just to get him acclimated to the students and staff. Woods really liked the content and quality of the newsletter and told Marqueth to pat the newsletter club on the back for a job well done. Mr. Woods had shared the newsletters with interested faculty at the Elementary School and interest in counting the ballots took care of itself. Including Woods, 14 people turned out to count the ballots. The committee dug into their task and each person grabbed a pile of ballots and a tally sheet. Within an hour, the job was complete, and the tally sheets were pooled into a single count. Out of 314 ballots, clear favorites emerged.

The faculty member recognized as Outstanding Peabody Teacher was Mr. Murphy. No reason was attached to the ballots, but "Murph" gained quite a bit of visibility from starting up the Newsletter Club. In addition, Murphy was just a great teacher that had a gift for building composition abilities of his students. He was a very positive communicator and took a keen interest in his classes and subject matter. These traits spilled over into his stewardship of the Newsletter Club. "Murph" utilized a teaching style that crafted student thought by asking questions to truly clarify what went into the composition students were assigned. When it was all said and done and the students had their assignments returned, their papers were typically lit up with a rainbow of color highlights that had meaning for the students from a color key Murphy had developed over his decade of teaching. Green highlights were particularly of interest because that was how positive thoughts were communicated. A yellow highlight was intended to communicate "this is a good idea, but you need to build the concept better". Completely harmless, but the yellow prompt allowed a learner to retool their thoughts. Red, on the other hand, was intended to communicate that quite a bit of thought was missing from the passage at that point. Orange highlight only showed at the beginning of a paragraph since it indicated some type of transition was missing from the adjoining paragraph. This system was a genius approach since it streamlined "Murph's" critique and shifted the burden from the teacher to the learner and really developed an understanding of the writing process. Murphy's strategy helped the student to think rather than rely on him to edit the content which was a tendency for other teachers in the school. There would be no questions asked about the validity of the voting when Mr. Murphy was named as the first recipient.

A pattern existed with the voting for the Outstanding Peabody Student. The school newsletter was a built-in public relations machine. Mr. Woods and his ballot team were really surprised when two students ended in a dead heat for the student recognition. Not being familiar with the majority of the students, Mr. Woods did not draw any connection to the tie. Addie and Hank had exactly the same number of votes out of more than 300. Hoping to report a clear number one student, Mr. Woods tallied the totals for all students receiving votes and they repeatedly totaled 314. He had done his job, thanked his committee for their time, and drove the ballots and the totals over to Peabody School for Mr. Marqueth to deal with. Once he handed over the totals and explained the lengths he took to break the student tie, he began to turn and leave. At that point, Marqueth gave a little snicker snort before he shared the reason for all the outstanding winners. Everything came down to the newsletter and its value to the students in the school. Marqueth then muttered, "no real surprise here, this is all about the newsletter; advisor and co-editors". He then thanked Woods and sat down at his desk, rocking back in his chair as he processed the recognition, particularly for the two students. Marqueth thought to himself, "I guess there is some value in this Inclusion movement. Wonder what Hank could do in a general classroom instead of that special class on the edge of campus."

Awards were issued at the spring assembly the following week. In addition to acknowledging the Most Outstanding, Best Attendance, All A's, Top SAT Scores, etc. were announced and received a certificate, Mr. Marqueth saved the Most Outstanding awards for last. First to the stage was Mr. Murphy who received a nice plaque and a donated gift certificate to one of the local restaurants. Finally, the moment arrived when the Outstanding Student was announced. Mr. Marqueth called Addie forward first and she got a standing ovation from the students. Marqueth made comments and piled on the praise as Addie stood next to him and humbly looked at the floor. As he drew his accolades for Addie to a close, he then captured everyone's attention again with his comment that "We have more than Addie to applaud for her effort at Peabody School, we have a tie! Hank, please come forward." Addie's expression spoke a million words. Some students may have been disappointed to find out there was someone to share the stage with – not Addie. As Hank was wheeling on stage, Addie spontaneously started chanting "HANK, HANK, HANK" which took all of one Hank to draw in part of the audience which quickly took over her cheer and was picked up by everyone at the assembly.

Hank retrieved his certificate from Mr. Marqueth as a back story on Hank was provided to the school. Not great detail went into the recognition, but some of the tragedy he had endured was briefed. Mr. Murphy remained on stage after his award and he stepped forward to share some of the effort Hank put into the newsletter. Most of Murph's comments focused on Hank's expertise with the photos, but he was just as quick to commend Hank for his thoughts and ideas that built the content of the newsletter. Many students in the audience began to whisper to one another that they were surprised with Hank's ability to accomplish these responsibilities. Some sort of shook their heads as if to suggest that Marqueth and Murphy were covering up and making more out of Hank than was true. Finally, Addie stepped to the microphone. Hank had used his communication cards to notify her that he needed her help. Hank flipped over cards and utilized different sets of cards from his mobile desktop attached to his wheelchair. Addie interpreted the cards for Hank who initially stated "Thank you for recognizing me for this honor. Taking your pictures and building my thoughts into the newsletter text has been one of my favorite things to do at school. I want to thank Addie for helping me so much. She is my best friend. I could not *do this without Addie helping me, so I want Addie to......and* Addie began to choke up with emotion. She looked at Mr. Murphy who was familiar with Hank's communication cards. After whispering in his ear, Addie walked off stage and was nowhere to be seen. As Murph took over the interpretation he spoke for Hank and said "*so I want Addie to have my certificate. I am really lucky to have a position on the newsletter, but I could not do any of this without Addie helping me.*"

Mr. Murphy reached over and gave Hank an awkward shoulder hug since he hadn't figured out how to shake his hand without looking desperate. Murph looked out over the audience and reflected on Hank's gesture. "What a noble gesture on Hank's part to offer his award to Addie. This is the type of person I have been pleased to get acquainted with through the newsletter operations. Hank has had to fight through so many things throughout his life and probably applies himself better than most of you in the school. I hope what you gain from this is to take a second look at Hank. Take a second look at everyone in this school. We all tend to get caught up in who we see and jump to conclusions about ability. This school would be a better place if everyone applied himself the way Hank does. Hank, I appreciate that you want to share your award with Addie. I am confident that Addie would not take your award. I am also confident that Peabody School is fortunate to have two students as good as Hank and Addie."

Mr. Marqueth stepped to the podium and redirected the dialogue from Hank and Addie to the school. "I couldn't agree more with Mr. Murphy and I feel like all of you in the audience knew what you were doing with your vote. I think we all understand our votes more now than we could have imagined. I am very proud to be the Principal for this school and want the very best for each and every one of you. That concludes our ceremony. I would ask one more thing from each of you. On three, let's have a big, loud "PEABODY" before we depart. One.....two.....three – PEABODY!!!

46

Tragedy..More Than a BeeGees Song

PARA had scheduled the monthly karaoke for tonight. This was to be the last special event until the fall. I really was looking forward to seeing all the buddies I had made from the previous PARA excursions. What a blast!

Seth and Lorraine threw me a curve this time. I am glad they thought enough of me now and respected my place in making family decisions. They had been invited to a Families and Disabilities meeting in Birmingham and asked me to accompany them. As Lorraine explained it, my presence and my wheelchair would help other families start to realize how we needed to make special efforts to meet my "needs". That sort of makes me cringe, but it is the truth. Both of them had really started to come around and better understand me in the past few months. So much of that was due to my involvement in PARA. On top of that, this was Karaoke - so come on, really, you think I will pass on that.

The option was provided to attend Karaoke and Caroline Sears would take care of me until they got back from Birmingham. Call me shallow if you want, but this was a no brainer decision. I am going to Karaoke and if I get extra time with Caroline, that is icing on the cake.

Seth and Lorraine loaded my light, portable stroller and me in the car and made the quick trip to PARA headquarters. I was unloaded and hugged more times than I thought was necessary, but these are my new parents and the glow was still there. It's not like I wouldn't see them in a few hours. **Finally, they made the walk to the PARA doorway and held it open for me to enter. We were a little early, but Caroline was there and set up had begun. Lorraine thanked Caroline again for offering to take care of me and for everything she had done for me and with me. Caroline very thoughtfully noted she needed to finish preparations and assured them both that she could handle everything. They made their exit after another couple of hugs and headed for Birmingham.**

I am having a blast at Karaoke! Wish I could sing out loud, but for now, this Barry Gibb is rolling through my mind:

Here I lie
In a lost and lonely part of town
Held in time
In a world of tears I slowly drown
Goin' home
I just can't make it all alone
I really should be holding you
Holding you
Loving you, loving you

Tragedy
When the feeling's gone and you can't go on
It's tragedy
When the morning cries and you don't know why
It's hard to bear
With no one to love you
You're goin' nowhere
Tragedy

When you lose control and you got no soul
It's tragedy
When the morning cries and you don't know why
It's hard to bear
With no one beside you
You're goin' nowhere.........
February, 1979

I did not see the realities of this one hitting home.

Seth and Lorraine made the rounds at the parent meeting and were fortunate enough to meet a number of parents in similar situations. Similar, but not the same. Every family has their own way of dealing with a child with a disability. Some families don't deal, and poor decisions are made. Frustrations can mount up and break a family in half. Other parents just seem to have a gift at dealing with the unexpected and becoming stronger when dealing with adversity. They met families from both extremes and many in the middle. It was a good night for the Grissoms to evaluate and adjust. The program had come to an end and Lorraine and Seth were anxious to get back to Hank. They learned a lot from the other families at the program, and one thing they learned was how much it meant to have Hank in their family. Time to get back to Tuscaloosa.

Lorraine raced to the car behind Seth. The rain shower had started out light enough, but as soon as they decided to make a run for it, the drops got thicker and just poured down in a torrent that made it hard to see the car. They ripped open their respective doors and dove inside. Doors were pulled shut and they laughed lightly together at how soaked they were. Nothing could take away from their evening and building their confidence to provide for Hank.

Seth cranked the engine and flipped the car into drive. They buckled seatbelts as they rolled across the parking lot before entering traffic. The windows began to fog over just a bit as their breathing was heavier than normal from the sprint from the meeting hall. Seth pulled out on the road toward I-59/20 heading back to Tuscaloosa. Lorraine was particularly excited about some of the programming that was shared from another parent she met and couldn't wait to tell Seth about it. This program sounded like a real opportunity for Hank to take the next step into adulthood. Seth pulled onto the highway from the ramp. This stretch of road was a 60 mph speed zone, but with the rain pouring down limiting visibility he kept his pace at 40 and reached to turn on the lights – "might need these" he thought to himself. It was state law to turn on lights when wipers were in action................WHAM!!!!!!

Seth's lights were a half second too late. Not to say the semi was not at fault, he was flying along at least 70 miles an hour and with the rain did not make out the car ahead on the road. In addition to the slower speed of travel, traffic was backing up from "Malfunction Junction". If you ever traveled through Birmingham on I-59 coming from Atlanta, you were very much aware of this stretch of highway. As I write, this particular slice of the highway is undergoing a major overhaul to eliminate the extreme twisting and turns in the midst of a constant flow of traffic. I-65 north and south intersected near this spot to make the traffic even more dense than should be tolerated. The rain, the curve, the intersection of two heavily traveled highways was the perfect storm.

The trucker had glanced down for a second to check his gps and when his eyes returned to the road, taillights were illuminating the next stretch of road as far as he could make out during the heavy downpour. At least they did not agonize in their death. The truck hit them full force without any braking which slammed their car into the next vehicle and like a line of dominos, one car after another rammed the rear of the next. The force of impact also spun their car sideways minimizing any benefit the air bags might offer. Seth and

Lorraine were T-boned by the truck and sandwiched between the semi and at least 10 more vehicles with each impact slowing the collision but compressing their vehicle. The semi had actually rolled up on top of their vehicle crushing it every direction possible. Highway patrol officers reached the scene and immediately knew that no one in that vehicle survived.

The vehicle was such a mess when all the dust had settled, it was very difficult to determine the make of the car. Patrol officers were able to read the license plate, called in the number, and determined it was Seth and Lorraine in the accident. Information on the deceased was withheld until notification of next of kin, but the evening news picked the story up and the broadcast filled in enough details to explain the fact that Hank was left stranded at the PARA center after Karaoke.

Caroline Sears was used to hosting participants from PARA events and Special Olympics competitions that she coached. Typically, this was determined in advance and Caroline would plan for the provision of care. In this situation, she jumped into action to comfort Hank and minimize his anxiety. Caroline talked to Hank and filled in as many blanks as she deemed necessary stopping short of drawing her conclusion that Seth and Lorraine were killed in the auto accident. She simply said that his parents were delayed, and it would be best for them and for Hank if he just stayed with her for the night. Hank took things in stride as they were presented but was limited in his capacity to interact. In the haste to leave PARA and drive to Birmingham, Hank's communication board was left in the car.

Caroline had begun to build Hank's capacity to interact using his iPhone. An interface had to be developed to help Hank express himself through Siri. Commands from the hard copy communication system destroyed in the car had been duplicated for iPhone use. As unlucky as Hank was to lose his second set of parents, he was fortunate to have someone that had backed up his communication patterns. A Computer Engineer student at The University of Alabama was recruited to program an app. Programming the app allowed Hank to choose a command and one or two keyboard selections to prompt Siri to talk for Hank. Hank could make a few elbow bumps on his control stick to trigger select commands through a short code designating full sentences and thoughts. This new generation of Hankspeak would become invaluable to Hank.

47

WARD OF THE STATE

Déjà vu, Hank's parents are taken from him in another horrendous fashion. Caroline and a social worker were to meet with Hank in the morning after she woke him up, got him ready for the day, and made him a good breakfast. Before the social worker arrived, Dr. Mugota and Dr. Marrell stopped at Caroline's home to help her break the news. All three people cared for Hank like he was their own child, but the matter of fact was he was not. All three people had their doctorate in special education and understood Hank's condition, but none of them were prepared to communicate this type of news. They each took turns giving Hank a hug and unfolding the story of the accident. Knox Marrell was strong in his faith and assuming the fatherly position within the trio, broke the news to Hank. Dr. Mugota followed up with assurances that Hank would always be able to rely on his network within PARA and that she was shocked just as much as Hank was to be dealing with his needs. Caroline had already done a lot to comfort Hank by taking him to her home and providing immediate care, but she knew there just weren't any words that would make this pill any easier to swallow. Hank took things in but struggled without his communication board to express himself to this assembly. If he could have talked, his thoughts would have bubbled through his tears.... *Oh God in heaven, what did I do to deserve this? Seth told me you would never give me anything I could not handle, but I don't know where to begin. Worse yet, people do not know where to begin for me. Caroline, Trianna, and Knox are so considerate, but I do not know what to do.*

Hank did not have next of kin available to take care of him in the U.S. In fact, Hank did not have next of kin back in Columbia. Hank was on his own, unable to care for himself, hardly capable of speech, and thrown into an unexpected situation with no way out. Protective Services from the Department of Children Services had been made aware of this new orphan as a result of the car accident. Given her background in special education, Caroline was aware of the network of state supports as well as her professional responsibility to report Hank's circumstances. If Caroline took in every child or youth in special circumstances, she would be the state agency. Her decade of work in special education had hardened her enough to follow through on the declaration to get Hank services, but it didn't mean she felt good about handing Hank over.

Ida Vinton pulled up to Caroline's home and approached the front door. After ringing the doorbell and being invited in, Ida set down on a couch near Hank. She was very matter of fact with her responsibilities and came across very cold with her deliberate explanation of life for Hank. He had no relations and as a result, he would be taken over by the state of Alabama and placed in an agency. Due to his lack of mobility and no speech, he would begin his new life in a supportive medical facility as the state sorted out Hank's future. *Wait a minute, I don't even know you and you are telling me what you are going to do? You listen to me; I don't want to go to your facility. I don't want your matter of fact attitude. Caroline, jump in here. Help me!*

By this point in the discussion, Caroline was holding back tears and limited to "Hank, I am so sorry. There is nothing I can do." He didn't have his communication system available, but she could read his eyes and knew his thoughts. None of the three professors could react. Ida had told them up front that this was going to be hard, that Hank was not going to be happy about things for a while, but the best action was to just rip the bandage off the situation and start his adjustment. Knox was fuming with the way Ida spoke to Hank and you could see his hands turn into clenched fists. His emotions were boiling through his body and he knew better than to start speaking because once he began to unload, he would lose control. Trianna sat back in her chair and just braced herself by squeezing the arms of the chair. She had experienced a lot of different circumstances growing up in Kenya and serving on local agency boards, but this was altogether different. Trianna did realize she needed to help Caroline pull back from the role of mother she had morphed into overnight in particular, but over the many PARA events when she had befriended Hank, Lorraine, and Seth. As Ida rose from her chair and got behind Hank's wheelchair, then she announced "Let's get this over with".

She began to push on the handles of the chair which offered up significant resistance. Ida had been through all kinds of child custody arrangements, but this was the first time without any parent fighting her and with a "client" in a wheelchair. Ida had experience with kids that refused to talk, but she was about to find out what happens with a client that couldn't talk. Her business first demeanor came to a screeching halt when she couldn't budge the wheelchair. "Unlock the wheels." she commanded. "Let's get a move on. Sitting here is not accomplishing anything." *I wouldn't move this chair right now if my life depended on it. I may not have my communication board, but I know what I want, and you are no part of what I want.*

Knox had diffused most of his anger as soon as he saw Ida experience defeat. She had not built any relationship with Hank and Knox knew that was key to any progress. "I suggest you step outside for a minute so we can help Hank handle things" said Knox. "Our experience with Hank is critical at this point in time and you need to leave."

Thank you Dr. Marrell! Someone needed to put her in her place, and you did that. I am so confused right now that I don't know how to handle this. I just need a friend, and you are a friend.

Trianna excused herself from the group and walked outside to confront Vinton. Trianna was very professional, but very straightforward with Ida. She let Vinton know that her conduct may be an efficient way to handle picking up a new member of the "ward of state" club, but it was far, far from effective. Trianna invited the social worker to leave and after some hesitation, Ida climbed in her vehicle and pulled away. Dr. Mugota returned to the house and found Hank conforming to a certain degree with what was occurring. Most of his composure was from shock. Hank was pretty numb but did understand some of the trauma process from the loss of his birth family.

All three of the faculty members informed their respective offices that they would not be available today. Knox called in an order and picked up lunch for the foursome to eat at Caroline's house. Caroline made a set of fundamental YES, NO, THIRSTY, BATHROOM, HELP communication cards to bridge the gap in Hank's missing communication set. Once the lunch had been complete, they discussed the situation and continuously posed questions that would allow Hank to take control of his immediate future. He was aware of medical needs that really exceeded the authority of these three kind souls. Hank was also aware of the fact that everyone except himself had daily responsibilities to address. He was handling matters in a mature manner, at least on the outside. Hank was still in shock from the tragic news and when coupled with his limited ability to express himself, came across more composed than he felt.

Over the next couple of hours, he was able to direct them to take him to the assisted living center after stopping to retrieve his personal belongings and most immediate supplies from Seth and Lorraine's home. He expressed his understanding and willingness to get to the facility and orient to his new way of life. Everyone disliked what was occurring, but they all realized the need to start the adjustment. Caroline took over transporting Hank to his home, gathering his essentials and clothes, and shuttling him to CentrePoint Life.

Caroline felt inadequate because she could not be a more directly responsible caregiver, but she knew the facts. Knowing the facts does not make the transition any easier, but she had been in similar situations before and respected the facts, even if she did not like them. Trianna placed a call to Ida Vinton to inform her that Hank had processed the situation and Hank had decided it was best to move into CentrePoint Life. Short and to the point with little opportunity for Vinton to say much of anything.

48

A New Group of Friends

It was official, Hank was declared a ward of the state and placed in CentrePoint Life Care Facility. CentrePoint was located on the edge of town in a remote location from most housing. The grounds were mostly natural landscape and offered a very peaceful setting for people deserving therapy. This was a multipurpose residential treatment facility for persons needing extended medical intervention outside a comprehensive hospital environment. With respect to Hank's support, the Centre provided temporary life care for persons with developmental disabilities as well as support for persons with Alzheimer's and/or dementia. A new population was recently added to the grounds in the form of youth with behavior disorders.

Once Caroline had unpacked Hank's bags at CentrePoint Life and had him settled into his assigned room, she accompanied Hank to a few of the surrounding rooms to attempt some introductions. Caroline felt it would be best if Hank had a few names of other residents at CentrePoint Life before she left. At least she would feel better about things if Hank needed a support person. People in this particular wing of CentrePoint Life were a mixture of medically dependent youth and adults that could not live alone or were in some need of medical support short of full-time nursing or medical staff. Hank was of the "can't live alone" type and he was actually somewhat comforted to see others in the same plight as himself.

One of the first residents Hank would meet was an older gentleman named Ray. Ray was in need of a dosage regiment of antibiotics that required him to reside in CentrePoint Life. He also was a high-level quadriplegic that for his stay in CentrePoint Life remained bed ridden. Hank would get names down later and build them into his communication system. Caroline did help Hank and Ray strike up a conversation to introduce Hank's communication needs. Caroline explained her position in Special Education at the University and described the beginning of the tech driven communication system being designed for Hank. Discussing Hank's background with Ray was just easier for Caroline to deliver. As Hank's story played out to Ray, it was clear that he empathized with Hank and would probably become a go to person. He was in his mid-60's and had been in the wheelchair his entire adult life. Ray shared his athletic accident in high school which limited his mobility. Initially, he was able to navigate in a manual wheelchair, but in the past decade, the overuse of his arms to push himself deteriorated his shoulders and he had moved into a power chair. Ray commented that he and Hank were driving the same set of wheels which brought a smile to Hank's face. Caroline excused them from Ray's room and accompanied Hank to meet more of the residents. Ray told Hank to come back any time and teach him more about his communication system. Hank rocked forward and backward, and Caroline told Ray that was his personal sign of agreeing and saying yes.

Caroline found a common television and game room with many residents taking in the day. Hank met a couple more people similar to himself that dealt with cerebral palsy, Vinnie and Melanie. Then Caroline found a couple other people, Bart and Ginny, that were closer to Ray's diagnosis with a spinal cord injury rendering them immobile without a wheelchair. Vinnie and Melanie were more capable of speaking compared to Hank, but they both had some type of voice inflection that really made them sound peculiar. *I would trade either one of them for their voice,* **thought Hank.** *Although, probably have to be Vinnie, that Melanie is pretty cute, and I would want her to talk back to me. Wonder what room she stays in?*

Every one of the people Hank met were in a wheelchair and seemed to be accepting of their lifestyle. The chaos of the last day was still pretty fresh, but it seemed that the novelty of a new location and so many new friends may help him through the accident. He made a mental note to deal with the cards he was dealt and not to get down. Easier said than done, but the proper attitude can go a long way.

In the past year, the ownership also began to take in youth with behavior disorders that were ruled by the court to be placed in a remote facility away from communities where they had terrorized the community. The intent was to circumvent juvenile detention and/or prison sentences. CentrePoint management saw the dollar signs and jumped at the opportunity to "serve" these youth. Hank began to make friends at CentrePoint just by sitting and watching television.

As Hank became more familiar with other patients in the facility, opportunities began to emerge that allowed for greater expression. One activity Hank really enjoyed was playing on an oversized checkerboard. His gross motor movement was developed enough to control his arm to shove the game pieces with his hand from one square to another. The irony of his interactions at CentrePoint focused on actually communicating with other people, many who had been written off as ignorant and dependent on someone else to exist. Hank was surrounded by social outcasts who were also misunderstood and underestimated.

One of his buddies was Bart who would seek out Hank every opportunity possible. Bart could get himself out of bed but required a wheelchair to navigate the hallways and open doors to recreation and greeting rooms. Bart was much older than Hank, probably 3 times Hank's age, and Bart was a talker. He came across as talking to himself, but it was just a coping mechanism he had developed over time. When no one answers your talk, you talk to yourself. Bart talked himself through every movement he made. Bart was a checker player too and introduced Hank to the game. Bart was an open book when playing checkers and his verbalizations helped Hank to develop a strategy.

If Bart was moving a disc across the board, he would tell himself why and, in the process, he taught Hank to play. "Slide to the right and protect from the side." Bart told himself. "Ohhhh, you moved into an open space for me to jump you", Bart grinned while he jumped one of Hank's pieces. "Crown my red", Bart thought out loud as he navigated across the board. "Now I can move anywhere", he gloated out loud. *Enjoy it while you can Bartie Boy, I'll be king of the board soon,* Hank thought to himself. Sure enough, Hank was an easy win for a week, but after continuous chatter from Bart talking his way through games, Hank was able to corner and jump Bart easily.

"Bart, you need to get another game if you want to win again" Hank thought as he quickly cut Bart off of every move. "You are really good at this Hank. Who taught you how to play?" Bart muttered to himself not realizing he had been the teacher. Bart and Hank continued the matches and looked forward to time together every day. *"Funny how God takes care of you when you let him"* Hank reminisced after losing his family. Hank really occupied a different earth than most of us. Few people gave Hank a chance and glossed over his inner voice simply because he did not talk out loud to accommodate everyone else. Here was a classic case of someone with the greatest struggles and barriers making his own way while other people could express their needs, ask for help, and whine around

about the most trivial matters. If only others could spend a day in Hank's life, maybe the tide would turn. More power to Hank as he applied 150% of himself while others applied 50% of their ability and wasted opportunities on a daily basis.

49

Show Me the Money

Another wing of the facility spread out across from a central front door. That wing was currently under use housing a more troubled "ward of the state" and was occupied by youth with behavioral disorders. These patients were much more valuable to the ownership of CentrePoint Life. Contracts were active for the owner to serve medically dependent patients and behavior disordered youth. Medical needs cost more to board with even a minimal nursing staff and physicians on call to address administration of medicines and any medical needs that might be present related to the reason for referral. If the arising medical need was not related to the reason for referral, the patient had to be transported to a local hospital for treatment. Certainly not the most efficient system of care, but this kept the cost down for the owner.

Behavior disordered youth on the far side of the building had a team of orderlies and maintenance staff that attended to their wing. The orderlies was a term used by the owner in the contract to contain (suppress) behaviors and were more like bouncers for a bar than what one would characterize as an "orderly". A behavior specialist (retired teacher) was employed to provide management training to "fix" undesirable conduct. A psychologist was on call to address any immediate crisis behavior that may be harmful to the patient, other patients, and/or staff.

The central front door with the movie theater window actually served as a partition between the two populations. Medical dependent residents like Hank and Ray were separated from the more troublesome and mischievous occupants on the far corridor. The "professional care" staff were paid the least amount possible and the ratio of care provider and patient was always kept at the highest number of patients per staff.

An occasional shifting of custodians into orderlies on paper was one method of containing operating costs. Another was to place a patient with behavioral need in the medical need wing. Any opportunity to bring another behavior patient into CentrePoint Life governed admissions since the facility was prioritized to make more money. A clause in both agency contracts using CentrePoint Life allowed for occasional housing of populations in opposite wings to maximize operations. There was never a surplus of medical need patients, but the court ordered behavioral population would never be turned away and overflows were placed in the wing that Hank was assigned. This co-mingling of patients usually resulted in the medical need patients mounting an uprising to keep the "criminals" in their place. In the event a mixed placement occurred staffing had to move with them. This would require one of the bouncers to move with them for the time housed in Hank's Hall.

Past attempts to mix populations were so disruptive that the ownership realized that the staff in Hank's Hall would not satisfactorily meet the challenge. One of the bouncers would be reassigned to oversee the "criminals" but they would also be expected to work with the medical dependent patients to maintain the profits. These placements were temporary and scheduled when a patient had shown some degree of maturity and could be relocated to the medical need wing with the least problem. Their mere presence in the wing was enough to incite a riot simply because of the patient's behavioral history (or so perceived). Early attempts to place and supervise instigated the tagging of a custodian as an orderly to show supervision following patient. The major problem with that arrangement is that it seemed that no one told the custodian they had extra responsibilities. In the event an overflow placement occurred, an orderly from the behavioral wing moved with the one or two patients and a custodian working in the behavioral wing was tagged as an orderly. The behavior disordered patients were not the type to organize any complaints and the management got away with the personnel shuffle.

50

Vanishing Act

Processing the loss of a second set of parents is tragic enough, but with Hank's unique background and limitations, some of the details got lost in the transition. Hank really did not have an appreciation for the wealth he possessed and did not think about Mr. Travers. He had so much to address just to live and get oriented to a new environment, the attorney was not on his horizon.

Travers, on the other hand, heard of the accident and passing of Seth and Lorraine. He attended the funeral service and was somewhat miffed not to hear any mention of Hank. Leon assumed for the week between the accident and the service that Hank was also in the vehicle with the Grissoms. Launching an investigation into the whereabouts of his young client did not seem appropriate during the service. Leon did wonder just where he would start looking for Hank. Adding to the confusion was a decision from the Life Centre to shelter Hank from the service to help him adjust to the confines of the facility. Once again, Hank's inability to communicate left him out of the decision.

Leon Travers was dumbfounded by Hank's absence from the service. "Who has Hank?" he thought. After the service, Leon mingled with the church crowd and approached Chuck and Marie, a couple that had delivered part of the eulogy for the Grissoms. Chuck made the delivery and reflected on the pride Seth and Lorraine had taken in planting the church in La Quiebra. He commented about picking them up at the airport and the enthusiasm the Grissoms had espoused when they reunited. From their comments and the emotional state they were in, it was pretty apparent that they were very close to Seth and Lorraine. Hopefully, they could shed some light on the whereabouts of Hank.

"Hi there," Leon said as he approached Chuck. "My name is Leon Travers and I worked with Seth and Lorraine to establish some accounts for an adopted son of theirs, a young man named Hank. They had adopted Hank during the time they spent as missionaries in Columbia, South America. I don't know how to address this any other way, but I cannot figure out where Hank happens to be. Would you have been familiar with the young man and where I can find him?"

Chuck looked like he had been run over by the truck, too. "Oh my goodness, with all the trauma and focus on Seth and Lorraine, I had let their son drop out of my consideration. Since they returned from Columbia, I had not spent nearly as much time with Seth. They were really quite busy with getting reoriented to the U.S., the community and the church. In fact, since their return, they had a very busy schedule visiting other branches of our church reporting their accomplishments and recruiting new missionaries. But yes, this is a real concern. Where is Hank?"

Chuck drew Marie into the conversation with Leon. "Honey, this is Mr. Leon Travers, he is an attorney that had set up some trusts and accounts with Seth and Lorraine for their son Hank. I am embarrassed to say that Hank really fell off my screen. Had Lorraine mentioned anything to you about Hank's activities that will help us find him?"

"Oh my," Marie declared. "This is terrible. I had really connected with Hank at the airport, but with their schedule of testimonies, we had not shared a lot. I do recall Lorraine mentioned a community activity group that Hank had gotten involved with. Lorraine was very enthused with how unique the organization was and how much of an impact they had on Hank. I had actually hoped to visit with her on one of their evening activities. I believe the organization was serving families and individuals with mental problems. Hank had trouble communicating but Lorraine said he just thrived at their meetings where they would use Karaoke as an activity. The agency was with the City Recreation department. In fact, they would hold events at the different community centers. Yes, the activities were organized by the Parks and Recreation, I think they advertise as PARA. Let me know if I can help further. I feel terrible that I had not given thought to little Hank."

"Thank you, Marie, that is the best lead I have so far," said Leon. "I will let you know if you can play a role resolving this. This is the most bizarre thing I have experienced. How could someone just vanish."

Leon spent the remainder of his day at his computer exploring community services. He turned his attention to PARA and the next day dropped by to meet with the director. He said he was very familiar with Hank and was really hurt to hear that Seth and Lorraine were in the accident. From what he knew, Dr. Caroline Sears of the University of Alabama faculty had played a large role in Hank's integration into the PARA social events. Caroline was a consistent presence in many PARA activities, and she had developed a strong relationship with Lorraine and Hank. Leon got contact information on Caroline from the director and set about taking the next steps.

Travers cut across town to the University and found Dr. Sears office in the department annex under renovation in the newly purchased Bryce property. Leon was pretty familiar with the campus from some of his clientele and appreciated the fact Sears' office was in a more remote part of campus. If you have ever been on a university campus, the most difficult part of navigation is parking within a mile of where you need to be. Caroline's office was near a decent parking area and his walk was only a couple a hundred feet to the building. Locating her office was unfortunate compensation for the parking proximity. With the renovation in progress, office numbers were out of sequence or non-existent and the building layout was nothing less than a maze. By the second office drop-in for directions, Travers was finally able to locate Caroline Sears.

Caroline was seated at her desk out of sight from the doorway and in the process of pulling together her work to take with her for the evening. Leon had just made it in time. After a knock, knock on the doorframe, he piped up, "Dr. Sears? Are you Caroline Sears?"

"Why yes, to whom do I have the pleasure," Caroline replied.

"Hello Dr. Sears, my name is Leon Travers and I am a local attorney in need of some assistance. One of my clients has seemingly vanished off the face of the earth, and my leads have brought me to you. Would you happen to be familiar with Mr. Hank Grissom, a young man dealing with cerebral palsy?" he asked.

"I certainly do know Hank, what a tragic event for his folks. I really need to check in on him and see how he is doing in his new location," replied Caroline.

"I agree, that was a very tragic circumstance, but I am glad to hear that you know where Hank is residing. I thought I would see him at the funeral service, but to my surprise, he was not present," explained Travers.

"Oh my gosh," said Caroline, "that is terrible, but his lack of communication does tend to leave him out of the circle. Now that you brought that up, that is not right. I should have been more vigilant. He was immediately declared a ward of the state and placed in an assisted living center. Hank is now a resident at CentrePoint Life services off of Veterans Boulevard. I actually helped move him in and get oriented. Once he gets around other people with disabilities, he just realizes a comfort level that made me feel comfortable too. I realized his adjustment was pretty quick considering the circumstances and I thought best to leave him for his own adjustment. Now I feel terrible."

"That is certainly not my purpose to make you uncomfortable. I have jurisdiction over some of Hank's assets from Columbia that will need some attention. In fact, you seem like a likely candidate to serve as part of an advocacy committee to assure proper use and investment of his assets," explained Leon. "That is getting the cart in front of the horse. At the moment, I just really need to see Hank and assess his circumstances."

Caroline pulled up the address and phone for CentrePoint Life facility and wrote it down for Leon. She handed the note to Travers, then volunteered, "And yes, by the way, I would be happy to serve as an advocate for Hank in any way I can. I see so much that Hank can do if we can just continue to develop his system of communication. He just needs to be able to express himself, and the absence from the funeral is evidence of what can go wrong. Let me know what and when you need me to do something."

"I will get back to you on the advocacy, right now, just need to set eyes on Hank," he replied.

51

Row, Row, Row Your Boat

Ray looked forward to Hank visiting him in his room. Since the Centre was located too far from family members, he only saw them once a week. An awkward silence was part of Hank's visit since Ray had to get accustomed to 64 questions to get to know much of anything about his little sidekick. What would have been a negative interaction for most people was pretty stimulating for these two. The longer they spent time together, the more fluent the communication. Ray got more adept at asking questions with Yes or No answers that built upon one another. Hank was able to lead some questions with pictures he found in magazines from the television room. In addition, Dr. Sears had continued to sophisticate the iPhone communication system and had spent time once a week orienting Hank to operating the system. Every visit she would leave with some new ideas to streamline the app.

As Hank became more proficient with the iPhone speaking for him, he could reveal more and more about what made him tick. Ray was really impressed with Hank when he tripped his iPhone system into action the second day. Before long, the two of them were cutting up and the age gap evaporated.

"How you have to be in bed all day and night?" Hank fed his iPhone with his broken English.

"Well Hank, I cannot walk, and I have developed some infections that keep me out of my wheelchair. I am in CentrePoint so I can get my medication. Once I beat this infection, I hope to return to my house. I have a wheelchair pretty similar to your wheels," Ray answered. They had already understood what happened to the Grissoms. Ray was a little confused with Hank's natural family from South America.

"You like not be here? You like house more?" asked Hank.

"Some things are more convenient here, but I prefer to have my own house and mostly my own schedule. My house is nearby, but it may as well be in another country," reflected Ray.

Hank felt like he had found Seth again as Ray became more versed in the experiences and tragedies he had endured. Ray really seemed relieved to have someone to interact with and time just flew by as the two new buddies dug deeper into their pasts. Hank began to fill in some gaps from his life in Columbia. Ray knew that Hank lost his family and had been adopted by the missionary team, but he didn't know any details. Hank divulged that his family was lost to a murderous drug dealer. He explained that this sicko was a guy named Faustino but went by the name *The Snowman* which was completed with a tattoo on his inner forearm as an identifier.

Ray was hanging intently to the story of drug dealing gone bad and how his new acquaintance was spared death. Details of the story were almost hard to believe, no they were unbelievable, but how could someone as sheltered as Hank make up a story like this? They chatted back and forth for quite some time, particularly with Hank's limited communication. The more he shared; the more convinced Ray became that this incident was legit.

Hank had pretty much described the vicious attack on his family to a point Ray was getting upset. Hard to imagine someone as fragile as Hank living through an ordeal like that. Making matters worse, a second set of parents had been taken away from him. Ray confided that he was pretty disturbed that anyone would have to experience a murder, let alone something that extreme.

An orderly brought Ray's dinner in for him. That was a cue that the discussion was over. If Hank was not in his room to receive the meal, there was a chance it would not be left. At the door, he toggled his control and spun the chair around to face Ray. Then Hank used his iPhone to ask if more of his friends from the tv room could visit with them in Ray's room. Ray didn't think about the request but just assumed the more the merrier.

Melanie, Bart, Ginny, and Vinnie randomly started to drop in Ray's room the next day. Hank immediately began to introduce his associates. Melanie was special to Hank from the moment he had met her. The past couple of days he made sure to constantly run into her. He thought she was the cutest and funniest girl he had ever met. Strange that he really had only listened to her talk to other people before he arrived at his conclusion. Bart was his checker partner who was a good sport about losing to Hank with greater consistency every day. Ginny, a friend of Melanie and inseparable; if you got one you got the other. Vinnie was a master on video games and owned a lot of them, so what better qualities would a friend have. Bart was closer to Ray's age than Hank, so he sort of balanced out the room in that manner, but he had a tendency to follow discussions rather than lead them. Ray caught on to the interest Hank had in Melanie and quickly started to nurture things along for his bestie.

Over the course of the next week, it was pretty common to have five residents enter the room to talk with Ray and among one another. Some of the voices from the newer members of the talkathon required some acclimation on Ray's part. He had given up on assuming they were saying nothing out of the newfound respect for Hank's intellect. There was no telling what went on inside someone's head just because Ray couldn't understand. He thought back to the many times in malls or in the community when people would talk loud to him as if he couldn't hear because he was in a wheelchair.

Everyone takes communication for granted and when the other person has an obvious difference, like a wheelchair, this snowball starts to roll down the hill getting bigger and bigger. Ray is paralyzed from the waist down so people assume he must not hear, and people will yell thinking that would help him understand – quite a leap. I have very little motor control and cannot walk or speak, so I am intellectually disabled – bigger leap. SIGH! Wow, off the soapbox and back to the gathering in Ray's room.

So, the CentrePoint Social Club is in high gear when the day-shift manager passes by Ray's room. Obviously in the midst of a bad day, the manager lit into the entire group and told Ray he had created a fire hazard by hosting so many "wheelchairs". "What is going on in here? Do you realize there is an occupancy limit on individual rooms?" the manager snarled.

"We were just getting to know one another. I have had more people in here before. You are just jealous you weren't invited," snapped Ray.

The rant went on about blocking the door and the unorthodox parking of their chairs. Ray laughed in his face since he was a customer in this partnership. Once the manager threw his hands in the air and left, the group came up with an orderly placement of chairs. Ray would call out "DETAIL" and the group became quick at placing two chairs against the bed facing Ray, two more chairs at the foot of his bed, and Hank in the right-hand man position on the far side of Ray's bed. With the command "LOCK" everyone knew to lock their chairs to maintain order in placements. Ray could call out "WHEELS" and everyone knew to pivot their chairs and exit his room in an orderly manner. Problem solved.... except Ray is stuck in bed in the event a fire actually occurred. Where is the management when you need them?

Ray's brother Jim was in town and stopped by for a visit. Over the course of their visit Ray had mentioned soreness building up in his shoulders from lying in bed all day and not getting any exercise. Once the words were out of his mouth, he knew he should have not mentioned his discomfort.

Jim had actually built Ray a walking station shortly after his injury. While enrolled in a welding class in college to become an Industrial Arts teacher, Jim had designed a set of parallel bars to help Ray stand up from his wheelchair. The entire system involved installation of a garage door track in the ceiling of their basement and suspending a parachute harness he bought from a local Army Surplus store. The harness was attached to a roller that he salvaged from a discarded garage door. Being the good sport he was, Ray actually tried to use the device with Jim's help. The effort was more wishful thinking on Jim's part since it lacked any method of moving Ray's legs other than Jim physically doing the work. Jim had hoped to continue stimulating Ray's muscles with the contraption. This effort was over 40 years ago, yet both maintained visions of Ray dangling in the parachute harness. It was as if he had been snagged in a parachute drop onto the church steeple in some little French village during World War II. Every war movie had a G.I. snagged in a tree or hanging from a steeple hoping the Nazis would not look up. Ray really appreciated the effort, but they both agreed it was not feasible.

"So, these sore shoulders", Jim asked, "would some range of motion activity help you?"

Before he really thought this through, Ray answered, "Well yeah, but I am stuck in bed and don't have a way to get to any equipment." Almost on cue, as soon as Ray replied, he looked up and could see the hamster wheel for a brain that Jim used activating at full velocity.

"On second thought, I probably will be able to move around more in a week or two when my treatment is complete" Ray injected into the conversation. Typically, a good action was to unplug brother Jim before he got the idea in his head. Too late. They chatted for another 45 minutes and Jim took off and indicated he would be back in a day or two……. he had an "idea". "Doggone it" Ray muttered with an eye roll.

It took Jim two days to pull together the equipment to "help" Ray. In his mind, Jim saw a rowing machine strapped to Ray's bed as a way to move his shoulders around while rowing. No need to wait two weeks for discharge, besides, discharge is usually longer than you expect. So, Jim strides into Ray's room early the second day with two oars complete with the mounting brackets from a rowboat. The brackets have been fitted with metal hose clamps Jim bought from the hardware store. "Wait 'til you get ahold of this" Jim announced. "I know this may look a little suspicious now, but just give me a chance to tweak this thing and we will get those shoulders loose." There was usually no way to stop him once he starts so Ray just laid back and watched the circus unfold. Jim fastened the hose clamps to the bed rails loosely to get the right fit for Ray's reach. Ray continued to play along for lack of any other options.

"You know they will not let me keep oars attached to my bed, don't you?" Ray contributed to a one-way discussion.

Jim was into the task and humming away like any mad genius would. "Once I refine this and we go to market we are gonna be rich. These bed rails are much more than just something to keep you from falling out." Now Jim has this grin of satisfaction on his face and Ray is just slowly running his head back and forth in a NO motion. "Voila……let's take this for a spin" announced Jim. Begrudgingly Ray started to row the oars.

"There is no resistance, this is not gonna do anything" Ray moaned.

"Ahhhh, that is why I brought the bands" Jim replied as he retrieved some rubber exercise bands he had at home. These were different colors to designate different tensions. Jim tied the yellow in a loop around the oar handles just below where Ray held on. The band made the oars cross in an X at the loop and Ray gripped the right oar handle with his left hand and vice versa for the left oar.

"Now you have resistance!" Jim stated emphatically.

Ray was actually surprised with the introduction of the band that it was working. Dang....Jim pulled one off. "But it still looks stupid and I am gonna have a problem with the management." When in operation, the paddle portion of the oars actually swung out away from the bedside about a foot and a half. If he got grief for the disorganized wheelchair parking, he was going to get a full citation for oars on his bed. Ray wasn't enamored with the treatment he received so these "problems" were really kind of sport for him to get back at the Centre.

"Not to worry" Jim replied. "Just tell them to give me a couple of days and I will modify the oars, so they won't be so conspicuous" as he stepped back and marveled at his contraption. "Can't you see how useful this will be for people stuck in bed like you have been for almost a month. These babies will sell like hotcakes!"

Jim pulled together his tools and pulled out one more piece of equipment for Ray. He found a 5-pound mini kettlebell weight at home that he thought might help Ray. When Ray was injured, his hand dexterity was compromised which eliminated grasping objects with his middle to little finger. He still had a pincher grasp which would allow him to grab this weight and get some arm curls in and possibly triceps extensions. Jim set the weight on Ray's mattress and hit the doorway.

"Oh my god" Ray thought to himself. He grabbed the oars and put in about two minutes of moderate rowing then realized he was actually getting some good out of this. A half hour later, the Social Club started to wheel in for today's gab fest which included the same question after question after question….."Whatzzat?"

52

DOING BUSINESS AT BUSINESS

The Snowman had taken his position at CentrePoint Life a few months ago and was assigned to the behavior disorder wing. This was not what he had in mind when he took the job, but he was not bothered by the behavior these young men displayed. Other orderlies had started work and were intimidated by most of the residents on this wing. Faustino knew what threatening behavior was and feared none of these kids. He had to keep his impulse in check so as not to fall back into enforcer mode, but he could dish back the trash talk. Bev had the sense that Faustino was pretty rough around the edges and might be able to relate to the youth. She actually considered he may be therapeutic to their cause. Bev was on the money with rough. He was a black belt in rough, but therapeutic was not in his DNA.

Most of *Snowman's* orderly peers were pretty much walking in place and their lack of life initiative was worn on their sleeve. These people included some do-gooders who felt a "calling" and just knew they could straighten out the delinquents housed in this wing of the facility. Most orderlies fell into the classification of "I just need some cash for food and rent" and clearly had no calling controlling their lives. In fact, on occasion, an orderly more desperate than others would speculate on *The Snowman* looking the part of a drug dealer. More than once Faustino was approached by someone looking for mind alteration. "Do you smoke?" was a frequent come on to Tino - while on a break smoking a cigarette. "C'mon" thought Tino most of the time, "let's not be so shallow." One orderly in particular was persistent enough that *The Snowman* allowed a thaw in his demeanor and came as close to befriending the guy as possible, without befriending the guy.

Faustino flashed back to his younger years and his life on the bottom of the food chain. After all, *The Snowman* did continue to ply his drug trade and after a couple of years in the States, he was beginning to build out his network. Rod just pushed and pushed Tino to allow him some product. "I bet your weed is pretty powerful?" Rod would question affirmatively.

"You carry any snort?"

"How about some powder?"

"Got anything I can shoot?"

Rod was not going to give in. His user intuition just compelled him to seek Tino out on breaks and his line of discussion always centered around some drug use. Closing in on a month of pestering, *The Snowman* finally caved in hoping to shut Rod down.

One of the associates dropped by the grounds of CentrePoint to drop off payment to Tino from a delivery. Tino asked his carrier if he happened to have any "samplers" with him. This was a rhetorical question since all of his runners had a "party pack" in their vehicle or were capable of producing small amounts within an hour of request…..it was just part of the business. Jonesie stepped away from Tino for a half minute and returned with an ounce of marijuana and a small baggie of cocaine containing enough for a dozen hits. Both substances were bagged separately then placed in a single freezer bag together. Tino placed the freezer bag on the ground at the inside of Rod's front passenger tire to make an exchange when they clocked out. After tossing the bag behind the front tire, he gathered some leaves to cover the baggie being careful not to disturb the immediate pattern of leaves close to the tire. He learned years and years ago not to make a cover up more conspicuous than a natural ground pattern. The leaves were collected from the side of a car three spaces away.

After work, Tino and Rod met at Rod's car. After asking for payment, Tino worked around the car, stooped down and retrieved the stash. He awarded Rod with his requested substance and pocketed the payment. *Snowman* thought that would be enough partying to keep Rod at bay for a few weeks, hopefully a month. Maybe he would go away.

A week later and Rod is all over Tino at the Centre. "Martino, that was some sweet stuff you got me. Need some more. My buds loved that powder and those leaves…..that was chill. Line me up man!"

"Hold on Rod, that was supposed to be your stash and for a month. Share with your buds? How many buds you talkin' 'bout? You didn't tell them where you got it did you?"

Silence and Rod looking at his feet.

"Did you??" *The Snowman* scowled as he already knew the answer. It really wasn't a question. "Not cool, this is not cool. That trade was supposed to stay here with us. You crazy? We both can go down on this. Man! I knew I shouldn't trust you." *Snowman* is in total melt mode with this revelation. "I will get with you later. In fact, we need to be the last out the door this evening. Meet me at your car after work. I need to clear my head……stupid….."

Rod went about his work like a robot, moving but totally withdrawn from the delinquents he was supposed to oversee. This wasn't a real departure from what he typically did, but Rod was somewhere else in his mind. "What did I do? I did not see that coming at all. What's the big secret with Martino?? I have bought stash before and most of the supply chain appreciated referrals. He must be having a bad day. Yeah, bad day, simple as that. But he was hot…..hmmm, not my problem." But it was Rod's problem and he knew it. The fire in Martino's/Faustino's eyes would not leave Rod's mind and he was in adult sulk mode the remainder of shift. Speaking of shift, this week Rod and The Snowman were bumped back to swing shift from 4 p.m. to midnight. The overnight crew would straggle in as late as 12:15 a.m. and the swing shift was not to leave their post until the incoming crew handed each person their timecard. A predetermined night staffer was partnered with Rod and a separate staffer was partnered with Faustino. Fortunately for Tino's partner, they were on time. As luck would have it for Tino, Rod's partner ran about 10 minutes late this night.

Rod punched out his card and left the building. He slowly made his way to his car. The Snowman was parked three spaces behind Rod's car so he could see this rat leaving the Centre. As Rod approached his door handle, Tino flicked his running lights on and off quickly. Rod barely noticed the flash, but the enforcers were looking for the signal and quickly jumped out of the dark, grabbed Rod, muffled his mouth to minimize noise, and dragged him to a remote canopy of trees. The beating was largely to Rod's torso and away from his face. Enforcement knew better than to leave markings that would get attention at work. If Rod limped a little or winced if moving something heavy, like a resident, that was up to his explanation. Inquiring about facial disfiguration was not a desirable outcome of a beat down. As a final threat from the crew, a large knife blade waved in front of his face with the point menacingly approaching his eyes. Rod was on the ground and much as he tried to push the back of his head underground, the earth just wouldn't move. The blade tip was inserted into his left nostril making the smallest cut to the outer ridge but piercing the interior surface of his nose. Rod was bleeding more than he realized, but it would wash up before tomorrow. Pain did not vanish nearly as quick as the blood would clean off.

This exercise in drug righteousness lasted about two minutes but seemed like hours. Both enforcers grabbed Rod and pulled him to his feet. Before he could get his footing, they dragged him over to their vehicle, shoved him in the open trunk, forced a wadded rag into his mouth while zipping his hands behind his back. Rod's veins felt like they would explode out of his forehead. He felt bad the rest of his shift after talking to *The Snowman* - now he wished he could just feel bad. One thug told him to enjoy the ride and get ready for some action then slammed the trunk lid shut. The other enforcer had already made his way to the front seat and revved up the engine. As the passenger door closed, the car shifted into gear and they pulled out.

After about five minutes of bumping around in the trunk, Rod was about as sick to his stomach as he could remember. "Was this sick from bouncing, or sick from anxiety" as Rod realized he was about to be killed? Smoother pavement must have spread out in front of the car as the trunk ride began to settle down; this was a dead anxious sick. As the foxhole faith began to kick in, Rod suddenly started praying to God, "Lord, be with me. Save me from this terrible situation I have gotten into. I am so sorry for the poor choice I made. Please, please save me oh Lord. I will never do this again"

The trunk popped open and both men grabbed an arm pulling Rod out of the trunk. One thug was still brandishing a knife to keep Rod squirming. Their orders were simple and straightforward, "Take this delivery and bring back the payment. $350,000 due at exchange. House is third one from the corner, 819, down there on the left. Porch lights are off because we ask not to be visible. We will be waiting here inside the car and can see you every step of the way. Try anything funny and it will be your last act of stupid. Do your job and we let you drive back in the seat instead of the trunk. Screw this up and the trunk is the last thing you will see."

Rod hustled to house 819 as marked by the mailbox at the street. After climbing a half dozen steps that seemed like a million, he knocked on the door. Within a few seconds, a gaunt, creepy looking guy opened the door and waived him in. Inside the front room he was greeted by three other men and two women that all appeared to be strung out and high already. Rod didn't feel comfortable with this whole set up, but he wasn't expecting to be in this predicament and just wanted things to end - alive. The creep handed over a satchel full of cash. "It's all there, trust me, I do not mess with *The Snowman*. As ordered, bundles of $20s and $50s totaling $350,000. Count it if you want, but I have double and triple checked. No way I am gonna cross that dude".

As quick as he had made it from car to house, Rod returned to the car. Attempting to avoid another trunk ride, Rod opened the rear driver side door, tossed in the satchel, and took a seat. He pulled the door closed and locked the door thinking it would prevent anyone from pulling him out and turning him into a spare tire. His stomach was in knots and he really wanted this nightmare to end. Rod shoved the satchel over the front elbow rest separating the front passengers.

"You did look in the bag to see the cash, right?" grumbled the passenger seat thug who was now pointing a pistol with a silencer at Rod.

"Yes, yes, I looked in the satchel and saw that the money was bundled and there was plenty of it. That junkie said he would never cross *The Snowman*, whoever that is, so I trusted him. I did what you told me. You didn't say to count it. I have never seen that much cash ever! If it is short it is on them, not me. Please, please, believe me. I handed over your delivery and retrieved the cash. Pat me down if you want. All I have on me is my wallet and car keys. Please, take me back to my car. I did what I was told."

DriverThug cranked the engine, threw the car into gear and slowly pulled away from the curb and nosed the car into the street. There was no traffic at the time. He actually drove with all lights off until they made it around the corner and into the next neighborhood.

Lights on and about a 15-minute drive back to CentrePoint. Rod was somewhat familiar with this section of town which helped him gauge time and distance. Returning to the facility in this car seemed like a much shorter trip than being stuffed in a trunk.

DriverThug pulled into the parking lot at CentrePoint and remained at a dark end of the parking pad. "Don't look back, don't memorize our license, and do not confide in anyone. We will contact you the next time, but if you run your mouth, you are done……trust me……you will be real done."

Rod unlocked his door, stepped outside the car, stood frozen next to the vehicle as it backed away and drove out of sight. "What am I supposed to do? Count to 100?" He took a couple steps then crumpled to the ground feeling like he was about to throw up. Rod took a couple of short breaths, then a deep breath, then raised up to a kneeling posture and swiveled his head to make sure he was not under any additional attacks. He finally stood all the way up and cautiously walked to his own car; Rod became very aware of his surroundings. "Contact me the next time? What does that mean? What have I done?" Rod thought it may be better to just die and get this over with - "What have I gotten into?" He drove home so he could lay awake in bed all night waiting for Ninjas to smash through his doors and windows.

53

Unexpected Encounter

Two new residents were assigned to the Centre which overloaded the hallway. Faustino was designated to accompany two crossover residents that he was familiar with from the time he hired on. Both boys had shown significant progress in identifying and bringing their behavior under control. Far from prepared for discharge, but both would benefit from being moved from the wing and the constant exposure to the daily threats and outbreaks that happened weekly. As loosely as the behavior wing was supervised, most residents just learned new tricks from one another. More than likely, these particular residents were more dangerous after life at the Centre than when they arrived.

Phil and Harvey were the two reassigned behavior subjects. Phil liked to be referred to as Flip and Harvey didn't really care to be referred to. Their new rooms were at the end of the medical support wing and about 4 doors down from Ray's room. In order to appease the medical residents, Flip and Harvey had to wear ankle bracelets that would set off alarms if they left their rooms. Faustino was seated on a folding chair immediately outside their doors with the understanding he would respond to the needs of the medical residents if requested. *The Snowman* was very compliant with his extra charge since most of the time it was transferring people from bed to wheelchair or back. Petty things like picking objects off the floor that fell or changing sheets if residents were out of their room was a way for him to pass the time on his shift.

The remote and isolated location of the Centre was exactly what Faustino was looking for to conduct his drug smuggling. *The Snowman* really did not touch the drugs, but instead met with the runners and collected payments from them. His role was all about the money and he had begun to sophisticate his US network after the first year in the country and getting established. It was about the time he began working at Smokeez that he would actually meet with his locals. Any time one of his rank and file showed up there, he got really uncomfortable. Now that the exchange and orders could be issued from the grounds of the Centre, Faustino was much more assured when meeting his men.

Faustino had taken measures to cover his tattoo with long sleeves when working in public, but the Centre was not public in his mind. He bought a few sets of scrubs to wear to the facility to work and loosened up with all short-sleeved tops. The amateur snowman tattoo was on display for anyone to see. After all, who at the Centre would have any idea what the tattoo stood for. Piece of cake!

The second day that the crossover placement had been made, Hank was heading toward Ray's room when he came upon *The Snowman* with his insignia blazing in the open. It was a chance encounter in the hallway, Hank was older and bigger than he was when Raul and Faustino murdered his family, and Faustino would never have thought to look for Hank. What were the chances – none. Faustino did not recognize Hank, but Hank knew what he saw. Hank's heart immediately started to race, and he felt sick to his stomach. He ducked his head down to avoid making eye contact and accelerated his chair away from the orderly and wheeled into the television room. *What the heck was that? No one other than The Snowman would be stupid enough to draw something like that on his arm.*

How could this be? It has to be that creep, the location, the image..... it was him no doubt about it. Same height, same build, crazy hair color and a bushy beard, but that jerk is the Snowman. He has to be. What do I do now? Sooner or later, probably sooner, he is going to recognize me. Then as if on cue, the orderly spoke to one of the staff down the hallway and that thick, sickening Latino voice confirmed Hank's suspicion. *I have to see Ray; he will know what to do.*

Hank wanted to hide himself the best he could. One of the residents in the room had a towel with him that covered his lap while eating snacks. Hank half-heartedly appealed to the "snacker" about using the towel and then slapped the cloth onto his head a few times. Hank was frustrated with the lack of hand control to cover his head with the towel. Good ole Bart was nearby watching his friend beat himself with a towel. Bart offered to help put it on his head since that is what seemed to be Hank's desire. He looked pretty strange, but Hank had his face mostly covered. He zoomed his chair into Ray's room and worked his footrest behind the door to push it shut. No one should hear what had to be spoken. "Hank, what's happening?" greeted Ray.

Hank pulled over to his regular position on the far side of the bed. He was frantic and had trouble controlling his arms but kicked his iPhone communicator into gear and began to describe the situation developing out in the hallway. His communicator was pretty much an R2D2 voice and inflection was not programmed. Voice inflection was not necessary when Ray saw Hank's face. This was distress to the nth degree and Hank's frantic movements only added to the climate. *"The killer is outside! I do not think he saw me! What can I do?"* Hank programmed into his iPhone. *This iPhone is in my way,* he thought. *"This is going to happen all over again. This time they will kill me. They will kill you too."* Hank continued to pull up his phrases.

Ray recalled from earlier conversations that Hank lost his family and had been adopted by the missionary team. Ray had not been able to erase many of the details from the murder, and now they were being brought back to life. He was concerned about Hank, but he was beginning to realize the need to be concerned for himself, as well. He was hearing that the very same mobster that took Hank's family was in the hallway. The world can seem small sometimes, but this was beyond comprehension. Ray's eyes bugged out. Hank declared that *The Snowman* and his unforgettable tattoo were back in his life. "And this creep is in the hallway!!! The Snowman works at CentrePoint Life."

Ray tried to maintain composure, "Okay, let's go back to the top Hank. Are you sure this is the same guy that killed your family? You really need to settle down," Ray said to reassure Hank that everything would be okay. "What is his name and what is his tattoo name?"

Hank shot back with a stern look that even he did not know was in him. It took him a few minutes since the name and tattoo were not front and center in his iPhone dictionary. Fortunately, Ray and Hank had discussed the horrendous attack on Hank's family, so some of the key content and names were in his iPhone dictionary. Hank labored through the selection of each letter until the system self-selected the name and activated the voice......"Faustino" ...... then ...."the Snowman. (pause) Danger." Hank couldn't shout through the iPhone, but the look on his face coupled with "he will kill me. He will kill us", convinced Ray this was very real.

Ray rolled the name Faustino back and forth in his head to make sure he got this right. Weird name, but different country. "Are you really sure about this Hank?" asked Ray. The absolute horror in Hank's face was enough to confirm to Ray that this was the real deal. "Now what am I gonna do," Ray thought to himself.

54

Awkward Meets Work

Rod returned to work at CentreLife for his 4 p.m. shift with Tino. On top of being zombied out from no sleep, he was scared to death that he might see Tino. Fortunately, they were assigned separate wards for the day with Tino spending time babysitting Flip and Harvey in the medical care wing. Rod finally calmed down after determining that he would be able to steer clear of what had turned into his DrugLord. Whether working side by side or in different wings of the complex, Rod dreaded an encounter and hoped he would not bump into Martino/Tino. Shortly after the beginning of hour two on the shift, the door to the reception area swung open and the two stood face to face and less than a yard apart. Tino shot daggers at Rod and did not say a word, but none was expected and no meaningful conversation was required. Rod's lower abdomen seized up immediately as he lowered his gaze away from Tino's penetrating eyes. In the process, he glanced down at the goofy tattoo on *The Snowman's* inner forearm. "Oh my gawd," thought Rod. "The junkie last night mentioned he would never, ever cross *The Snowman* and this had to be who he referred to, it had to be. If I only knew who I had been pestering to score a handful of highs, I would have definitely steered clear. This guy is more famous than Zorro. I am so stupid."

"Parking lot - tonite - same routine - be ready," Faustino muttered in a hushed tone. With that, he retrieved a magazine to read from his locker area near the time clock, spun around, and returned to the medical support wing.

Rod felt his stomach clench up even further. "This is never gonna stop. I'm doomed." He did the only thing he could at this point, he walked the opposite direction and entered avoidance mode. Just like a 3-year-old, Rod walked to the end of the hallway, buried his face in the corner, and began to swing his shoe back and forth softly kicking the wall. Kick and push, kick and push. Over and over Rod activated his straight leg back one foot from the wall for the next kick. He positioned himself in this repetitious state of worry for a good 10 minutes. His behavior was without thought, without purpose, and best of all, without consequence. As simple as this routine was - it had no value. Rod's consequence meter was pegged out after last night's mission and now, the threat of round two loomed over the remainder of his workday.

He thought about just walking out the door and going home. What would he do at home? Lay on the couch staring at the ceiling waiting for the door to bust in. He knew they could find him in no time. Last night was setting the hook. Tonight, they are gonna keep reeling "Rod the fish" in. "How did I get into this mess?" he thought to himself. "Better yet, how can I get out of this mess?" Rod hadn't eaten in 24 hours and he finally remembered what hungry was. Somehow that slid in behind worrying himself sick. He walked down to the vending machine and looked for the biggest pile of carbs and sugar he could find. One thing at a time and now was splurge on junk time.

55

Reeder to the Rescue

Cy was making his way to Tuscaloosa and communicating back and forth with dispatchers from the FBI. His specialist in data mining was on the phone. Cy was troubled with Martino vanishing into thin air, but confident that Josette had pinpointed his destination. There had to be some trail that Martino/Faustino had left, but he had nothing in purchases. Faustino had gone to "cash only" after charging his room at Motel 6. "Hmmmm.....what is the missing piece?" Cy thought to himself.

Cy asked the data mining specialist to run a search against criminal records and background checks throughout Alabama. By the time Cy had left Columbia and was closing in on Tuscaloosa, the database had coughed up a strong piece of info. No criminal records would tie to Martino Randolsa, he was an outstanding citizen in his own right. His wife had attested to his character as had his boss at the construction company. But a background check had been run by a step-down medical complex in Cottondale, Alabama adjacent to Tuscaloosa. A Martino Randolsa had applied for work at the complex and, working with people and disabiities, state law required that the agency ran backgrounds on everyone that applied for work. Martino passed the background check with flying colors. That was the best the data specialist could do. Cy had been preoccupied with all the closed ends in this case and was in deep thought in his drive. He kept going over and over the details trying to make sense of what he was missing. When informed of the background check and the location in Cottondale, a grin began to take over his face. This was too good. Cy asked the specialist to text him info on the CentrePoint Life location and he made a beeline to that facility.

Finally, an end appeared to be in sight. Cy drifted back to the notice of the Yamaha water cycle and the communications with some top-notch law enforcement in Medellin, Columbia. He could not help but think that he had cracked the code on this one. Big question in his mind, would this Carbona guy be employed where the check had been run on his alias? Oh, the webs we weave. Solving the cases were such a sense of satisfaction. He would prefer they were not tied to loss of life but putting the stop on a drug ring would at least attach some value to the family that had been murdered. Cy had no way of knowing that Hank would be sitting, literally, in the middle of all this and the young man had beat the FBI to the punch.

Unaware that Hank was scared to death with what he had realized, Cy settled in for the rest of the trip maintaining the speed limits as he followed the two-lane roads from Montgomery to Tuscaloosa. If he could foresee the dynamics at CentrePoint, the blue flashing lights would have been activated. Instead, with his mind finally settled on a strong clue to resolve the case, Cy cranked up his radio and caught some tunes on the way to the Centre. Not a fan of Country Western, he wasn't enamored with the selection, but the strongest reception seemed to be cowboy rock tunes. His left hand slid down the wheel to steering with two fingers while he stretched his right arm across the back of the passenger seat. Cy was pleased to see four-lane roads open up at Centerville to carry him the final 40 miles to Tuscaloosa. He popped the cruise control into 65 miles per hour and dreamed of bringing justice to another crook. Life was good.

Cy's navigation screen finally showed him within 5 minutes of the facility he was so desperate to find. Highway 82 from Centerville brought Cy into Tuscaloosa on the south side as it turned into McFarland Road entering the shopping section of town. The six-lane road carried him five traffic lights to Veterans Blvd. where he took a right turn. As he got closer to his destination, Cy began to sit up straight and lean into the wheel. He was getting anxious to find out if he was going to strike pay dirt.

56

Showdown at the OK Corral

Ray managed to get Hank somewhat composed when the rest of the Social Club began to roll into place. Timing was terrible, but with this crew, dismissal without talk would have been a disaster. Hank was already in place when Ray called out DETAIL. For some reason they all had the idea that they had to get to their original place in the lineup and every time the command was invoked, the chairs sounded like a demolition derby event. Banging and clattering but the four random members eventually got pulled into place. An eye roll would have been appropriate, but Ray and Hank had more pressing issues on their minds.

At the front door to the Centre, Cy had pulled his SUV into place and parked. He opened his driver door, stepped out, and strode to the entrance to CentrePoint Life. He approached the safety window and booth separating the wings of the facility.

Mary was at the front desk today and she looked up as Cy presented himself. He flashed his FBI badge to get Mary's attention. Mary did not recognize the FBI insignia, but immediately sat up upon seeing a badge. Cy explained his purpose and asked if a Martino Randolsa was employed by the facility. Without the least concern for confidentiality, Mary flipped through a directory of staff and announced that Mr. Randolsa was employed and on rotation right now. He had been assigned to the medical needs ward for the week.

She pointed to the right and said he should be right inside this door. "Let me buzz you in" as she released the security lock for entry. Cy opened the door, walked inside, thanked Mary and opened the door to the wing.

Ray decided that since *The Snowman* had not recognized Hank from the hallway, it may be best to use the element of surprise. Someone needed to say "this should never be attempted at home" but Hank had managed to get Ray worked up about this criminal being in their midst. Clear thinking was not the order of the day. When Ray gets mad about someone being mistreated, he gets MAD!! After a few seconds of contemplation, Ray directed the four buddies on the side and foot of the bed to pull back in a random manner to create a staggered path for an orderly to have to walk through. If he could get Faustino to answer a call to his room, he needed to entice the thug over to the side of the bed with Hank.

Ray had an adjustable rolling tray over his bed with a bunch of medicines and personal devices filling its surface. Ray shoved the tray off the tabletop toward Hank on the far side of his bed. Everyone in the Social Club except Hank was in a manual chair that they pushed with their arms. Hank's chair was motorized and very heavy from the battery pack that activated the motor. Just like Ray's chair, he knew that if Hank positioned his chair and powered it off, there was virtually no way to move the chair without controlling it with the battery. Once the chairs were in the locations he wanted them, Ray had Melanie who was closest to the door swing out in the hallway and call for Faustino.

Melanie swiveled her chair into the doorway and leaned out so her head was in the hall. "Help me mister" she called out to Faustino. *The Snowman* was flipping through a magazine and glanced up then back to his reading. "Please mister, we need some help in here."

Faustino reluctantly got up from his chair and tossed the magazine on the seat. It dropped with the pages spread open but lopping over the front lip of the chair. Ever so gradually the magazine inched over the edge as gravity did its thing. The magazine hit the floor just as Faustino got to the door frame of Ray's room. Melanie had retreated back into the room into her spot. Faustino spun around to see his magazine on the floor. A slight burn came over his emotions.

He turned back to Ray's door preoccupied with his magazine. This probably worked to Ray's favor. Faustino stepped in and muttered "yeah?" to the crowd. Ray replied "could you come over here and help me with the tray that fell? I need to take my medicine." As part of the plan, Ray's job was to get Faustino to the floor. The spilled tray was part of the floor. Ray told Hank that when he was down, Hank's job was to push *The Snowman* under his bed. Ray kept his bed raised high off the floor to give him a better view of his visitors. It was a guess on his part, but he felt like there was enough clearance to fit someone under the bed uncomfortably, but under the bed.

Faustino muttered something in Spanish and Hank bristled up. Faustino still had not registered who Hank was as he stooped to gather up the multiple objects scattered on the floor. Before *The Snowman* had entered the room, Ray had already secured his best grip on the small kettle bell weight. Faustino was kneeling on the floor on one knee when Ray decided to confirm things once and for all…..he spoke in a controlled voice that would not startle the orderly but definitely get his attention if it fit - "Hey, Faustino" he said. *The Snowman* had just gotten his hands full when he heard his name and out of reflex looked up. As he glanced up at Ray, the 5-pound weight was launched square into his temple with Ray's left hand. With his right hand on the oar, he started slamming it down against Faustino's back and neck. Faustino was woozy from the weight hitting him and out of reflex fell flat to the ground with the thumping of the oar. When he hit the floor, Hank sprang into action and flipped his lever to drive his chair into Faustino's side. Poor little Snowman had no option but to roll under the bed as the feet on Hank's chair climbed over his arm and pinched the skin on his side. Hank flicked his control back and forth slamming Faustino as much as he could to corral him under the bed.

Take that you piece of crap, Hank thought loudly to himself. He could not voice things but was clearly getting some satisfaction out of inflicting pain on this jerk. *I hope you rot in hell for what you did to my family. For my Papi, for my Mami, for Carmelita.....take this.* The rage cursing through Hank's body started to produce tears in his eyes. Never in his wildest dreams did Hank think he would realize some justice over *The Snowman* let alone be part of physically taking him down. Hank was so proud he felt like he would burst. *Justice served.*

Faustino had made his way completely under the bed when Ray called out DETAIL and the onlookers slid their chairs against the bed blocking off any space large enough to let their capture loose. Then Ray shouted, LOCK and all chairs were set in place effectively immobilizing *The Snowman* under the bed. He did not have enough room to leverage himself against any of the wheelchairs.

The Snowman was not going to take this lying down.......well, he is lying down.....but he was regrouping to fight back. Tino understood from an early age that you always come prepared... not the Boy Scouts.... just his own motto. He had squeezed under the bed from all the ramming that Hank imposed against him. Tino centered himself under the bed to escape the footrest beating he had endured. He had very little room to maneuver under Ray's bed, but he did finally manage to inch his knife out of the holster in a utility pocket in his pants just above his knee. His pants had enough loose fabric bunched up at this pocket that no one had noticed him carrying his weapon around the facility. The extra space hiding his knife worked against him in this particular position. His loose pantleg offered no resistance to his knife holster to pull the blade free. For a moment that seemed like an eternity to Ray, Hank, and the Social Club - Faustino was motionless under the bed as he fished for the knife. *The Snowman* muttered away in his thick Latin accent but had to remain still to retrieve his knife. Once the blade was extracted from the holster and available for use, Tino had to reposition his arm to attempt his counterattack.

Fortunately for Hank, Tino's initial target for retaliation, his wheel sat and blocked the area where this thug could get the greatest leverage for his knife blade. The Snowman had to reach above his head to swing his arm parallel to the floor and down on Hank for any power thrust. Space between the wall at the head of Ray's bed and Hank's wheel was limited, but it was the best option to swing at anything Hank. Hank had pivoted his chair open with the feet toward the wall waiting for the next attempt for Tino to crawl out from under that bed. Hank had quickly realized that the greater swing in the movement of his chair and footrest, the more pain he could exert on his nemesis. *The Snowman* struck the tip of his blade blindly into the tire of Hank's chair. Tino was simply swinging wildly to cut anything with his knife. Not a lot of air was needed to fill the thin tires and the knife piercing the tire flattened it instantly.

Hank did not realize the flat tire immediately, but noticed a leg protruding from under that bed. Time to start bashing again, only this time the flick of his control barely moved the chair. The flat tire and weight of his motorized chair almost immobilized Hank's movement. He could still make his arc to jam Tino's leg, but it was in slow motion and ineffective. Tino was wriggling out from under the bed and gave the appearance of a mechanic on his back under the side of a car. Everyone knew that the commotion had slowed down, but everyone knew quiet was not necessarily a good sign. Hank was approaching panic mode and his body response was shutting down his capacity to regulate his motor commands to activate his iPhone. *What can I do now? He took my family, he beat me, he made me feel fear that I did not know existed. Now, he has returned to my life. Worse than anything, I have put Ray in danger and I literally cannot move. I cannot fight. I cannot respond. This is soooo wrong.* His flight response had taken over and physically, Hank was out of commission.

Ray and Hank made eye contact and his mentor realized the fear that totally consumed his young counterpart. Hank had a tear welling up in his eye as he pleaded with his stare for Ray to do something. *I am so, so sorry Mr. Ray. I had no idea this part of my life would ever resurface. I am scared - very, very scared and stuck. Please Ray, do something for me, for all of us!!* All Hank could muster was to look at Ray and roll his eyes down to Faustino wriggling from under the bed.

Ray caught the target from the roll of Hank's eye toward Faustino. This was going to be a blind shot; Ray could not freely pull himself up to locate *The Snowman* on his own. Ray channeled his best **Home Alone** attack mode, caught the five-pound kettle bell weight with the back of his right hand and shoved it under the bed rail. "Bombs away Hank, bombs away," Ray muttered to Hank as the weight edged over the mattress and dropped 2 ½ feet squarely into *The Snowman's* crotch. A better connection could not have been made if Ray had looked. As the weight smacked Tino directly in his manhood, he began to double up in the small space under the bed. The movement was involuntary, but it did connect his forehead with a thick intersection of angle iron supporting the mattress of the bed. Hospital beds such as the model Ray was living in had leg and back raise functions. *The Snowman's* forehead hit squarely on the frame and hinge assembly allowing for a bend at the waist for the bed occupant. Striking the frame created a piercing pain and almost knocked Tino unconscious. He was woozy and filled with extreme pain from his forehead to his crotch but managed to retreat back under the bed to recover. As his legs pulled back under the bedframe, Hank continuously nudged his control switch and gradually closed up the space that was vacated.

Ray eyed the bed controls embedded in the bed rails. The icons on that system showed a head up and down button, a foot up and down button, and a flat mattress up and down button. For some reason, these controls escaped his attention as weapons until now. Head and feet only pivoted the mattress from the horizontal axis of the bedframe. The mattress up and down was another type of control. Ray kept the mattress horizontal as high as he could to better meet and greet company and get the assistance from staff who could basically stand to medicate, clean, and attend to him. He hit the down arrow on the controller and felt his bed start to lower. Large screw fixtures at the head and foot of the bed began to synchronously churn allowing the frame to slowly track closer to the floor. Ray engaged the controller until he could hear Faustino begin to grunt from the compressed space and hear his breathing labor because he could not fully inhale to breathe.

57

Vigilante Justice

As if on cue, Cy Reeder popped his head in the door to see what the commotion was about. Melanie, Bart, Ginny, and Vinnie were frozen in their chairs suspended between fear and pride for Hank. They were speechless. Ray asked if the man could get some help. Cy finally noticed the person under the bed. "Do you need me to help this man under your bed?" inquired Reeder not really realizing how crazy that sounded.

"No, he needs to stay there but we need the police and quick" Ray shot back.

"Well I can do better than that", said Cy as he flipped his badge, "FBI".

Ray glanced over at Hank who was fully focused on the caged animal under the bed. "Unbelievable" Ray muttered. "WHEELS" commanded Ray and the social club pulled back and rolled out the door. "This thing under my bed goes by the name Faustino. He is a drug dealer from South America and his cartel ID is *The Snowman*. He murdered Hank's family....this is Hank here," as he pointed to Hank.

"Unbelievable" Cy muttered.

Ray began to raise the bed to allow Cy to pull *The Snowman* out for capture. As he fished the creep out from under the bed, Faustino positioned his knife upside down in his hand to cover the blade under his forearm. His grip on the knife handle would allow him to swing the weapon to cut with the blade swinging away from himself. Typically, your knife grip set up for stabbing and plunging the tip. In order to disguise as best he could, Faustino kept the blade against and under his forearm until completely pulled from under the bed. As Reeder reached to grab his collar to lift him, Tino allowed the blade to swing into the open as he took a swipe at the agent. He caught Cy pretty good with a gash across his shoulder and under his clavicle. It was mostly surprise and some pain, but enough to release Cy's grip on the shirt.

Tino fell back against the foot of the bed to catch himself then made another swing with the knife at Cy's face. *The Snowman* really didn't have his balance to accurately target the blade against Cy. The swing did cause Reeder to fall back against the wall and stumble to the floor. Tino shot out the door as soon as the opportunity arose.

Unfortunately, the Social Club membership was clustered outside the door in typical rubber necking fashion. Nothing like an accident or trauma situation to gather a crowd. Tino actually tripped over Vinnie's chair and fell to the floor. He scrambled back to his feet and latched on to Melanie's wheelchair for support. *The Snowman* triggered his criminal reflex and took Melanie hostage. Sometimes you need to laugh or you are gonna cry. Sometimes, you laugh in an inappropriate manner or circumstance. Nothing was funny about Tino taking a hostage but watching this hardened criminal attempt to back his way down a hallway hunched over attempting to pose harm to Melanie sitting in a wheelchair 2 feet off the ground was ironically humorous. As any wheelchair user is accustomed to do upon stopping, Melanie had locked the wheels on her chair to prevent her from drifting out of her desired position. In addition to being bent over and grossly minimizing his leverage, Tino was attempting to hold a knife against Melanie as a threat while dragging

Melanie and her locked chair down the hall. Everyone could see that Tino would like to start his hostage taking over with a more flexible hostage. Well, too far into hostage taking, you just have to dance with the date you brought to the party. Everyone within reach was in a wheelchair or bed ridden. The staff were either attempting to lock resident doors or to get behind a wheelchair and wheel people out of harms way.

People tend to underestimate the ability of people in wheelchairs, Tino was no different. Melanie may not have known any better - OR she may have been in an adrenalin driven rage - OR she decided to fight rather than be kidnapped. Maybe it was all of the above, but as she bit down hard on the wrist holding the knife, she simultaneously popped the metal arm of her chair out of its post. Quicker than even she expected to free the chair arm, her weapon was in hand. Call it luck, call it skill……..no, it was luck……Melanie swung the chair arm across her shoulder into the nose of *The Snowman*. More shock than pain from the bite, Faustino flinched hard and lost a full grip on the knife just barely hanging onto the knife by the blade, he really could not strike to cut anyone but himself. Once Melanie landed the chair arm to his nose, Faustino doubled over, dropped the blade to the floor and clutched at his nose.

Vinnie, Bart, and Ginny were not about to idly sit by when a friend was in trouble. They quickly wheeled into place, dislodged an arm from their own chair and joined the fray. Too many times the news headline reveals small crowds watching someone being attacked while no one helps, everyone just watches in amazement. Not this time, the Social Club took this jerk head on. Fortunately, no one knew who he was, that would have been reason to pause. In this situation, however, Melanie was in trouble and none of the trio hesitated. Each person picked out a different piece of real estate and began to vigorously chop away at *The Snowman*. His drug network members and his customer base may live in fear of *The Snowman*, but you have to know who the fabled terrorist is to be in fear ahead of time. He was in his scrubs, he was considered a staff member, but in this particular moment, he was hurting one of their own.

Ginny went in for one of his knees and got him to begin to bend down. Metal on bone was taking its toll.

Bart zeroed in on his wrists smashing his metal arm on the bones he could see in Tino's wrists and back of his hands. Collectively, Bart made it impossible for Tino to grab anything.

Vinnie had a laser focus on Tino's neck and head. Ginny and Bart were taking swings and making painful distractions. Vinnie was living out one of his Mature rated video games that the staff didn't know he had. Day after day Vinnie vicariously had watched himself in attack mode on zombies, terrorists, and robbers. Today was Vinnie's day to shine with some full force arm swings which slammed Tino at the base of his skull, on the crown of his head, and not intentionally but very effectively on his temples and eyes. Vinnie was a combat machine and in full assault.

With the support of her clan, Melanie was free to pay back as well. Surprisingly, Melanie was just as vicious as Vinnie swinging frantically at any piece of *Snowman* she could eye. On one wild swing, she caught Tino directly on the Adam's apple in his throat. That clearly hurt and dropped him to the floor again clutching his throat. She then just made a series of machete chops across his chest, on his hip pointer, then down the opposite leg from Ginny.

Lucky for Tino, Cy Reeder had made his way into the hallway with a pillowcase held over the only cut he had received. The Snowman was clearly subdued by the small army and Cy had to grab a couple of chair arms in midair to bring the vigilantes to a halt. He was also calmly telling them to stop. When Cy was convinced he was not going to catch one of these swings himself, he knelt down with his knee in Tino's back. With one hand forcing Tino's face into the floor, Cy put the FBI arm twist on him and cuffed him, one wrist at a time. Everyone in the hallway and most of the rooms could hear "You have the right to remain silent……." as Cy administered the Miranda Rights to Faustino.

58

Rod the Rat

The Snowman had gotten a decent taste of what he was so used to dishing out, and at the hands of the least expected. There was a certain beauty in the way this all shook down. Most of all, super sleuth Hank making the identification and herding *The Snowman* under the bed was pure justice. As Cy was shoving Tino out the hallway door and through the foyer out to his SUV, the captive was resisting as much as he could. Navigating two separate sets of doors in a restricted space allowed Tino to make considerable noise scuffling and kicking to keep his escape options alive. As the noise and commotion made its way through the Centre foyer and into the parking lot, the juvenile wing came to life.

It was not as if they were going to attempt a jail break, but every resident in the juvenile wing was pressed to their windows on the exterior wall watching this live takedown occur. Flip and Harvey had followed through the open door into the foyer and in a way, gave themselves up by asking to be returned to their wing of peers. They saw and heard enough that even they realized that crime doesn't pay, and they were going to behave.

As the attention shifted to the parking lot arrest, Rod decided to take a look too and was pleased to see that "Martino" had been discovered. For a minute, Rod felt a sense of calm and actually did a fist pump at his waist. Could this be a turn of fortune? It was late in the day but early in his shift. Rod couldn't help but hope they would catch the entire crew and remove the threat of life hanging over his head. Rod saw that Tino was thrashing around in the back seat of the FBI car and decided to approach the agent. He did not trust that Martino would have some way to alert his network, but he wanted to do what he could to come clean and get this drug monkey off his back.

Consistent with the rest of the unusual behavior occurring at CentrePoint, Rod made his own contribution to the scene. He had made his way to the front entrance of the foyer and was squatting down in an attempt keep *The Snowman* from noticing him motion to Cy Reeder. Cy had just finished the famous push the head down to push a criminal in an officer's vehicle. Tino was handcuffed behind his back and Cy had successfully harnessed him into the back seat with the seat belt and shoulder strap. Short of Houdini showing up, Tino wasn't going anywhere, but he continued to thrash around like a caged animal. Rod was in the open front door squatting and waving his arms to get Cy's attention.

Cy turned from the passenger side of his vehicle to get to his driver door by walking in front of the car. He would have had to been blind to miss Rod flapping his arms. Cy glanced back to the inside of his SUV to check on his cargo - still there. "What can I do for you sir?"

Rod replied, "No, it is what I can do for you. I know some things about that guy in your vehicle that I believe you would want to know. Can you come over here to talk just for a minute?"

Cy strode back to the front entrance and looked down at Rod. "Can you stand?"

"Officer, I really would rather not. I am down here to keep Martino from seeing me. I need your help in return for some information I can share with you. First, I need to know if you can grant me immunity."

"Well", Cy drawled, "attaching strings usually indicates you have something to hide. I admit, I am not at liberty to promise you something like you have asked. If you have information of significance that you are willing to release, we can typically make it beneficial to the source. I am not sure what you are talking about."

"Uhmm, I --- I --- I think I know about a drug deal."

"You THINK you know of a drug deal," Cy parroted back to Rod. "Thinking you know something and actually knowing something are two different things with different value to me. Care to go a little deeper? Or would you like to ride with us to law enforcement with your buddy in my transport?"

"Oh geez, I got pulled into his business and had no idea who I was dealing with. Not sure I even know who that is now. I will just admit it right now, and please don't jump me for what I am gonna tell you. I bought a couple of joints off that Martino there and shared them with some friends of mine. I am not sure why, but he got all bent out of shape that my friends enjoyed it with me. Last night when I was leaving work just after midnight, some guys jumped me and forced me to deliver a big pile of drugs for over a quarter million dollars. Like I said, I am not sure why, but they jumped me."

"First of all, what is your name and what does last night have to do with you groveling around now?"

Rod gulped some air, swallowed hard, and talked nonstop, "My name is Rod Foster and they dropped me off last night back here after beating me and scaring me to death and told me I had to do the same operation tonight and I do not want to go through what I had to last night and I want you to catch those guys too and I am not safe anywhere, anytime and this is too much."

"Dang, take a breath. That sounds like I would be interested Foster," replied Reeder. "Let me get this maniac booked in downtown and I will come back here to talk further. What time are you off and is that when this next drop is supposed to take place?"

"My shift ends at midnight and I will be forced to deliver a load if you don't save me. That is what I know, and can you keep me out of jail? If you put me in with him I, I don't want to think of what might happen to me. I am not safe," Rod replied. He was an open faucet.

"Alright, getting him booked in sufficiently in the local facility is gonna take about two hours. Lessee, 5:30 right now. Let me process him and pick up some equipment. I will be back here by 9 which will give us a few hours to address your situation. You'll be fine until then. Best thing to do is act like nothing happened, things need to settle down inside your facility. I will ask for you at the front desk by 9 o'clock."

Cy took care of booking The Snowman into the Regional Law Enforcement headquarters downtown. He shared the background on Faustino and wanted to make sure the locals knew what they were dealing with. No need to let up on the pedal and allow an escape attempt. Booking Faustino into the jail facility took just under two hours. Cy asked for the head of narcotics to arrange for some assistance that evening and to secure a tracking device to help monitoring the activity.

59

Rock, Paper, Scissors

Cy pulled into CentrePoint a few minutes past 9. As was custom, he approached the security window in the foyer, flashed his badge and reintroduced himself. Mary was still on duty and assured him she remembered who he was. Cy asked to meet with Rod Foster and Mary buzzed him into the juvenile wing. She said he should be available along the first section of the wing.

Cy pulled the door to the wing open and stepped inside. He walked down the hallway looking in each room to find Rod. He made it down six sets of rooms when he found Rod in one of the rooms breaking up a conflict. "Rod, when you get things under control, we need to talk. I will wait in the hallway."

In less than a minute, Rod was next to Reeder and panting like a dog. They stepped outside when Rod started his inquiry, "How you gonna do this? Whatcha need to know? Did you work things out for me? How you gonna do this?" he quizzed in rapid fire.

"Here is the way this will have to work," Cy responded to Mr. Innocent. "You are going to have to assist us in the bust. We need to make the arrest immediately after the exchange is made. You will need to ride with these guys just like last night and make the drop while picking up the cash. I have a tracking device here that is very small and will transmit up to a half mile. We can determine your location within 10 feet. You can carry this in your pocket, slip it inside your shoe, have it with you wherever you want to hide it, but you need this on you and active so we can follow from a distance."

"But I don't want to," Rod interjected. "This ain't fair."

Not batting an eye, Cy continued to explain, "I have a SWAT unit of 10 officers who will be involved in the surveillance. An unmarked car will engage the route of the vehicle carrying you and stay within a quarter mile of you at all times. Once your vehicle comes to a stop and we determine from the tracer that you have left the car, two SWAT team members will position within 20 feet of that car. The two members will already have entered the make of car and license plate into the legal data base. They will be able to take your leads down and secure them in seconds."

"Not fair, not gonna," blurted Rod.

Cy acted like nothing had been said, "The balance of the team will approach the drop house from the opposite direction. These 8 members of the team will surround the house in pairs at all doors. They will incorporate night vision equipment and be undetectable 20 feet away. At the front of the building you will enter, two pair will flank the entrance and quite likely be prone in the yard ready to enter when you exit. Members of the SWAT team will have a silent activation system informing them when you have exited the building with the payment. If there is a stairway into the front entrance, you are to take the steps down and immediately upon stepping to the grounds, drop to the ground on your stomach and one of the team members will cover you to prevent any harm coming to you. That person will have protective head gear and Kevlar protection which will shelter both of you. You are to push the container with cash in front of your head as an additional barrier should any munitions be discharged."

"Should any what be discharged?" Rod stammered.

"I anticipate this Team will successfully capture all parties involved in the drug exchange within one minute and typically without any weapons activation." Cy just barreled along. "As mentioned, you will be sheltered following the drug exchange and you are at low risk. Once the operation is complete, your cover agent will release you and we will escort you back to CentrePoint. Questions?"

"Not fair, not gonna, ain't gonna do it, thisizz 'gainst the law.... ain't it?" Rod ripped back at Cy.

Cy crossed his arms and cocked his head to the side, "You broke the law with the purchase of drugs, delivery of drugs, and receipt of a massive payment for the drugs. Seems to me like you will help us as described or spend some time in a local jail. You do recall who is currently in a local jail, correct?"

"Geeezzz.....that ain't right!" Rod grumbled pathetically. "Shoot, I am not going to that jail." Following an awkward pause and a deep breathe, Rod agreed, "Alright....alright. But what about me, what do I get in return? I can't stay around here with all *Snowman's* workers. So, what do you do for me?"

"Now we're talking," Cy shot back. "I have an approval to offer you witness protection and relocation. You will have to agree to return for testimony, but you will have full support and relocation from after the bust until trial. Once you have testified, we will arrange a more permanent relocation and new identity. Fair?"

"Fair," Rod mumbled. "I wanted to relocate right now, but I guess I earned it."

"You earned it." Cy said matter of fact.

Rod went back into the Centre and attempted to work. Pretty hard to focus on work when you are in the middle of busting a drug cartel, haven't slept in a full day, don't like your job to start with, and you have a strong sense that you could get killed tonight. At least he was going through the motions and it kept him occupied until the next steps.

Staff on the swing shift started to exchange cards to clock out. Rod's replacement was about five minutes late which bothered him this evening. A critical factor in the drug exchange was currently behind bars at the local jail. Would the threatened exchange occur tonight? Did his two new "buddies" know Martino was tied up for the evening? Will they act independently if *The Snowman* is not at work?

Rod stepped outside and began to cross the parking lot. A vehicle sat back in the shadows where he was mugged last night. Running lights flashed once when Rod looked at the car. "Am I supposed to go to them?" thought Rod. "Hmmm, only makes sense since the cops would have simply called things off if they were sitting in the dark. Guess I go to them." He pivoted direction and walked to the car.

Driver window was down and this was clearly the same car. "Get in."

Rod started to feel his stomach tightening up. He knew that running was not a good choice in the moment. He touched the handle on the rear door and hoped it would make the car disappear in a cloud of smoke. Hoping this was a nightmare did not happen. Door handle is real….check…..door swings open……check……

"Get IN !!" the driver demanded.

"Here goes nothing" Rod thought to himself. One gulp of air then he stooped and sat down in the car. The car was in motion before Rod's foot was all the way in the car and they drove off as he pulled the door close.

"Same drill as last night, but we spared the boxing practice. You are one of us now," grunted the front passenger.

"How much is the deal tonight?" asked Rod. This really didn't matter but small talk seemed to be called for.

"Smaller job tonight," the driver joked, "quarter million dollars for pure snow. They can cut it or pass it straight on. Just do your job and no one gets hurt."

At least Rod was feeling some assurance that they were unaware of *The Snowman* getting caught. He was not treating this like a walk in the park, but he definitely was emboldened with his assessment of the situation. Rod had the tracer on and in his shoe. He had gone so far as to pull the insole loose from the shoe and tucked it under the pad toward the center of the arch of the shoe.

The drive was west tonight then north into a run-down trailer park. Thick pine trees made a ring around the cluster of trailers which only occasionally had any outside lighting. Most of the visibility was from interior lights which were at least partially covered by window shades. DriverThug pulled to the far end of the trailer cluster with car lights off. He circled the car pointing in the direction they had come from. A smaller satchel was in the back seat next to Rod. "Five trailers up with the yellow bulb over the front door, nothing cute."

Rod opened the door and slid out with the bag. He seemed to get a little braver with each step thinking that this was almost over. He approached the designated trailer, stepped up on a single rickety platform and knocked twice. The door swung open and a heavyset man waved him inside.

"Set it down right there" as he pointed to a coffee table "and you sit down right there" pointing at a rattie looking sofa. "I will go get the money for after you demonstrate the goods for us." He strode down the hall of the double wide trailer and disappeared for a few seconds.

Rod felt his pulse pick up a quick step. This was not part of the deal. It appeared chubby man was here alone, but that was not a given. Rod thought that if he were making this type of purchase, he would definitely have some back up. The buyer lumbered up the hallway by himself.

"Here is a short straw, let me draw you a line to take." One of the packages was sliced open and a razor blade was dipped into the powder for the flat edge to be piled with the drug. The coke was deposited on a small flat tray with a tip of the blade then divided in half. Each of the halves were cultivated into straight lines characteristic of a user preparing to snort the drug.

Rod was trapped. Comply with the buyer and demonstrate the quality of the product, or refrain, do not get paid, and be subject to breaking up the bust that he was steering forward. When the driver said this was pure, did he imply unsafe to consume and needed to be cut? Not sure that the customer was armed or not, was he even safe to refuse the dose? Rod had to roll the dice on use or be on the street at the mercy of a large ruthless bunch of drug smugglers. He sat forward, accepted the flat tray and straw, and drew in the drug one nostril at a time. Rod felt the impact of the cocaine immediately. "Ahhhhh….that is some fine stuff. You are gonna like that coke. Wow! Let's finish this deal."

Rod took the payment in a crumpled paper bag. He glanced into the bag, sorted bills in bundles just like the night before. Without counting each bill, this payment passed the eyeball test. Actually, the amount of money was inconsequential. It was a significant payment for a large amount of cocaine which fulfilled the equation Cy and his SWAT would need to take down the immediate members of the cartel. Rod grabbed the handle to the front door then stepped outside. The drug was really starting to kick in now. He stepped onto the front platform then almost tripped stepping onto the lawn. Feeling pretty lightheaded, Rod fell to the ground as directed.

Like clockwork, the SWAT team went into operation. Rod's cover man was in place and jumped on him. The trailer only had a front and a rear door. Two were stationed outside the rear door positioned and ready to intercept if that door was opened. Three SWAT members jumped from the ground and forced their way through the front door just as a deadbolt lock was being slid into place. The receptacle for the deadbolt had already been partially pulled loose from the doorframe. Not many trailer doorframes are built to withstand

SWAT ramrod and this one was no different. The force of the ramrod busted the frame loose enough to disengage the deadbolt. The three members of SWAT barreled through the door and the first officer slammed into the portly customer knocking him to the ground. Easy takedown with no resistance as the handcuffs were locked into place behind the buyers back as he was administered Miranda Rights. SWAT members 2 and 3 worked their way down the hall pausing and clearing each room as they encountered a door. Everything checked out all clear. Three knocks on the back door signaled the two SWAT officers outside all was clear inside.

SWAT officers were on the rear corners of the cartel car. Once the front door to the trailer had opened, these officers were at the front windows of the car with the high intensity scope lights on their pistols pointing into the cab of the vehicle. The scopes were blinding and prevented the driver and rider from any aggression. Each door was ripped open and the thugs were pulled out and to the ground. Each man was flipped over, face down, and restricted with sets of handcuffs. Miranda Rights were administered.

Without elaboration, Rod sobered up the following day. Arrangements were made at Cy Reeder's direction to place Rod in Witness Protection. His new name and residence are unknown. Call him protected. Both thugs from the car were brought up on racketeering charges and convicted with a life sentence with no opportunity for parole. *The Snowman* was tried and convicted of the murder of Martino Randolsa in addition to drug trafficking. Faustino Carbona was sentenced to two, consecutive life sentences with no opportunity for parole. Carbona has been requested for extradition to Columbia for multiple charges of drug cultivation, distribution, and murder. That request is under consideration while Faustino is being held in a federal maximum security prison in solitary confinement.

60

Just Rewards

Sometimes life throws you a curveball.......and sometimes you hit it dead on for a homerun. One would be hard pressed to compete with the struggles that Hank endured and continues to deal with. But Hank now has his day, and much is turning up roses.

Cy tried to deprive Hank of the $2,000,000 reward for capture of *The Snowman*. He just could not get over the limitations that Hank had to deal with and was convinced that someone else had to have realized Faustino from the Most Wanted posters. After all, they were plastered in every U.S. Postal Service building and anyone could have matched the picture to this culprit; anyone but Hank, completely disregarding the role that the tattoo contributed to identification. Ray played a big hand in explaining and ultimately testifying on Hank's behalf. Mr. Travers worked in conjunction with Ray and secured the reward for Hank. For all the effort Cy put into the investigation, it really came down to Hank noticing the tattoo on Tino's forearm. Travers was asking that Mr. Reeder be removed from the FBI for showing the amount of bias and discrimination that he displayed toward Hank. Hank rose to the occasion and cranked up his iPhone communicator to offer another outcome. Hank asked for a simple apology from Reeder which he received. Hank went on to thank Cy and commend him for showing up when he did to take the captive into custody. Judgment of the reward was made in Hank's favor.

Leon also assembled a topflight advocacy council for Hank to make financial decisions on his Carlos-funded wealth. Drs. Caroline Sears, Knox Marrell, and Trianna Mugota all gladly agreed to work with Mr. Travers to assist Hank with explaining purchases he may need and investments he would make. Laurel Spain, the administrative assistant for the three professors, was placed on a retainer by Hank to assist him in communications and processing payments. Once the reward money was coupled with some smart investment strategies, Hank lived without worry for the remainder of his life.

Hank expressed what an outstanding and valued friend Ray had become in CentrePoint Life. In order to compensate Ray for what Hank considered, saving his life, Hank felt compelled to do something significant for him. Ray and Hank continued to see each other frequently and on one of Hank's trips to Ray's home, he made good on a gesture to pay him back. Hank had arranged for Leon Travers to clear Ray's mortgage and Hank handed him a copy of the deed free and clear. Ray tried to refuse the gift, but when Hank needed to win a discussion that he was already winning, all he had to do was turn off his iPhone communication system. Hank just sat with his endearing little smile plastered all over his face. Enough said!

Leon also successfully ran the house that Seth and Lorraine owned through probate and got that assigned to Hank as his home. Seth was not as forward thinking as Carlos with insurance coverage, but he did carry a $500,000 policy intended to pay off the mortgage and carry Lorraine through the initial years of life alone if something did happen to him. The policy had been put in place before the couple relocated to Columbia for the mission work. Hank was not a part of the family equation when the policy was drawn up. Since Hank was formally adopted by the Grissom's, he was entitled to the benefit payout in Lorraine's absence. Leon used his skills to assign those funds to clear the mortgage on Ray's house and leave an additional $250,000 for Hank, which cleared the Grissom Home mortgage.

Hank still struggled to comprehend the amount of wealth he had accumulated. As a method of leveraging Hank's resources, Dr. Mugota proposed a tax-deductible scholarship account that Hank could fund with a valuable return on investment. Hank needed assistance with transportation, medical needs, continuing education, physical and occupational therapy, and general support in his home. Utilizing the vast network of manpower development at the University, Dr. Mugota arranged for the scholarships to support a variety of student disciplines who could learn professional skills while they fulfilled the multitude of life needs that would help Hank thrive.

No one could deny that there was an ulterior motive to his gesture, but Hank wanted to enjoy life with some select friends from his time at CentrePoint Life. His new home was a three-bedroom, three bath home. Hank invited the four members of the Social Club to move in with him at Grissom Home. Melanie was clearly as happy to spend time with Hank as he was with her. Melanie was a sure commitment to take up residence in Grissom Home and benefit from the University students on scholarship as much as Hank. As noted previously, wherever Melanie went, Ginny went. So, Ginny and Melanie moved to Grissom Home as roommates in one of the bedrooms.

Bart was a bit older than the rest of the club and more set in his ways. Bart opted to stay in CentrePoint Life with visiting privileges to see Club members knowing that Hank would arrange transportation to and from both residences. Besides, he could never compete with Hank in checkers and needed to scout some lesser competition at CentrePoint Life. Vinnie was a different personality. He knew the assembly of videogames and was a master player, but a great deal of that skill resulted from his rigid need for structure. When he saw Bart decline the offer, Vinnie hesitated to make the move. Hank put together a top-notch video parlor in his house that was equipped with the latest of all the top three consoles and a dedicated 65-inch monitor for each system to broadcast. Hank was sure this would be the draw for Vinnie to make the transition. Initially, Vinnie made a trial residence at Grissom Home with the provision that CentrePoint Life would hold his room for a full week if the change did not work. Three days into the move and Vinnie was in full panic mode. His daily routine had been disrupted. Some people would look at the opportunity for independent living as the ultimate opportunity. Vinnie needed the structure, the routine, and oddly enough, the limitations of living in CentrePoint. He moved back to the facility, but any time Bart visited, Vinnie visited.

Bart and Vinnie were day visitors and never stayed more than one meal and four or five hours. The third bedroom was maintained with two single beds which were used by rotations of the scholarship students to provide 24-hour care if needed. Someone with a driver license and permit to transport residents of Grissom Home and CentrePoint was always on hand. Occasionally, one of the scholarship students found things so rewarding and educational, that they would take up residence and save themselves the expense of an apartment. Caroline was the point person over the scholarship participants and made sure that full semester residence was not free loading, and no one did.

Caroline, Trianna, and Knox were constant participants in the Grissom Home and looked for innovative ways to serve the three residents. The trio of professionals were gifted in improvisation and well connected with a variety of departments on campus. The housing model keyed off of scholarship resources was submitted for a national competition to design and replicate the synergy of resource and need that exchanged between campus and the Home as a residential model.

Finally, with some advisement by Dr. Caroline Sears, Hank proposed to Melanie asking her to be his wife. Melanie accepted his proposal without hesitation. A small wedding ceremony was held at Arisen Son Church with members of the CentrePoint Social Club serving as the wedding party. Ray gladly agreed to be Hank's best man. Mrs. Hank Grissom gradually became adept at finishing iPhone communications that Hank started.

Ginny continued to live with the Grissoms and learned many independent living skills from the rotation of scholarship students visiting Grissom House. Gradually, Ginny took over much of the house cleaning and cooking and was paid prevailing wage for a home assistant. Ginny didn't have any expenses other than her clothes, so her wage was invested in some mutual funds similar to the wealth that Hank and Melanie shared. Leon Travers assisted Melanie in her decisions. To this day, Hank and Melanie, with the assistance of Ginny live an increasingly independent life.

www.ingramcontent.com/pod-product-compliance
Lightning Source LLC
LaVergne TN
LVHW041701060526
838201LV00043B/516